the world through the eyes of **angels**

Middle East Literature in Translation
Michael Beard and Adnan Haydar, *Series Editors*

KING FAHD CENTER FOR
MIDDLE EAST & ISLAMIC STUDIES

TRANSLATION OF ARABIC LITERATURE
■ 2010 AWARD WINNER ■

Syracuse University Press and the King Fahd Center for Middle East and Islamic Studies, University of Arkansas, are pleased to announce THE WORLD THROUGH THE EYES OF ANGELS *as the 2010 winner of the King Fahd Center for Middle East and Islamic Studies Translation of Arabic Literature Award.*

the world through the eyes of angels

Mahmoud Saeed

Translated from the Arabic by
Samuel Salter, Rafah Abuinnab, and Zahra Jishi

Syracuse University Press

English translation copyright © 2011 by Syracuse University Press
Syracuse, New York 13244-5290

All Rights Reserved

First Edition 2011

11   12   13   14   15   16   6   5   4   3   2   1

Originally published in Arabic as *Al-Dunyā fī aʿyun al-malāʾika* (Cairo: Dar Merritt, 2006).

∞ The paper used in this publication meets the minimum requirements of the American
National Standard for Information Sciences—Permanence of Paper for Printed Library
Materials, ANSI Z39.48-1992.

For a listing of books published and distributed by Syracuse University Press,
visit our Web site at SyracuseUniversityPress.syr.edu.

ISBN: 978-0-8156-0991-9

Library of Congress Cataloging-in-Publication Data

Saʾid, Mahmud, 1938–
    [Dunya fi aʿyun al-malaʾikah. English]
    The world through the eyes of angels / Mahmoud Saeed ; translated from the Arabic by
Samuel Salter, Rafah Abuinnab, and Zahra Jishi. — 1st ed.
        p. cm. — (Middle East literature in translation)
    ISBN 978-0-8156-0991-9 (pbk. : alk. paper)
    I. Salter, Samuel, 1954–   II. Abuinnab, Rafah.   III. Jishi, Zahra.   IV. Title.
    PJ7862.A5236D8613 2011
    892.7'37—dc23   2011042807

Manufactured in the United States of America

The child is born an angel, then goes along behaving like a devil day after day; even if he leaves the world, he leaves it a little devil.

Mahmoud Saeed is a prominent and award-winning Iraqi novelist. He has written more than 20 novels and short story collections, including *Port Said and Other Stories,* which was published in 1957. The first military-Baathist Iraqi government seized two of his novels in 1963. Saeed was imprisoned several times and he left Iraq in 1985 after the authorities banned the publication of some of his novels, including *Zanka bin Baraka* (1970), which nevertheless won the Ministry of Information Award in 1993.

Samuel Salter is a writer and translator based in the Chicago area. He is also a published novelist under the pen names Sam Reaves and Dominic Martell.

Rafah Abuinnab worked and lived in Jordan most of her life, then came to Chicago where she studied and worked for the last ten years. Currently, she is teaching Arabic at DePaul University in Chicago. Rafah enjoys reading novels and poetry.

Zahra Jishi resides in Ohio. She has translated works by Mahmoud Saeed and Lotfi Hadad.

Preface

Mahmoud Saeed

This is the story of a child in the forties and fifties of the last century. It is the story of a people in a remote city very far from America, a story of ordinary people in one of the oldest cities in the world, Mosul. It is a city of stone, which blazes in the summer and freezes in the winter. It is the sister city of Nineveh of ancient history.

When I cast my mind back now, to remember how people lived at that time and compare it to their life now, I am swept up in a whirlwind of sadness and pain. Then people lived as brothers in total harmony, as if they were one family that included Muslims, Jews, and Christians. Because the city sprawls among fields on an endless plain, it was filled in the summer with Kurdish, Jewish, Turkmen, Aramaic, Yezidi, Shabak, and Armenian peasants. The hotels and markets were filled with them, as were the squares and alleys. Then they disappeared as soon as autumn hove into view, to leave the inhabitants of the city to themselves again, with their rituals of brotherhood, affection, and intimacy.

I have written more than twenty novels, and usually the writing of a novel requires a year or more of thought, but I did not think much about this novel. The idea came to me like a meteor shining in the sky.

Last year I went to Tijuana, Mexico. My heart was heavy with the griefs and catastrophes and battles and divisions and tragedies of my country, where everyone is at war with everyone else, and the country is a sea of blood in which all are drowning. Since the invasion of Iraq my mind had gone into hibernation; I had not been able to find the concentration to write a single word, and I realized that the road I was on led only to death.

And there in Tijuana I saw things that reminded me of Mosul in the summer. Brotherhood, crowds, gaiety, and people staying up late at night. Music in the public square, songs, food on push-carts in the streets, complete harmony, and boisterous life like the life of my country.

And then I saw something that has made the greatest impression on me since I came to America in 1999. I saw a child of about five, running barefoot, carrying a bag full of onions, tomatoes, oranges— I'm not sure. He ran with all his might, stopped for a moment to rest, and then ran again. I followed him; he went into a modest house and then came out, and in his hand was a small apple as payment for his tremendous labor. He sat on the doorstep of the house and began to gnaw on it with delight.

At the same age I was barefoot like him, running almost a kilometer to get to my father's shop before he had to leave for afternoon prayer. Then I would go back home when he returned. It made me happy even though I got no reward of any kind.

How, I wondered, could my family have let me run by myself all that distance without worrying about me? How did we live in such safety and confidence and happiness? I carried out that duty for eight years, every day until I was twelve. I don't remember that anyone ever bothered me.

This novel tells the story of a boy whose childhood was violated and oppressed by the demands of a cruel older brother before whom he was powerless. He spent most of the day catering to the wishes of a man who cursed him, starved him, and struck him for any reason or no reason at all, and burdened him with countless tasks that ended only at the end of the day. While other children were enjoying all kinds of games during the summer vacation, this boy had to run barefoot under the rays of a burning sun that produced temperatures in the shade of 110 to 125 degrees Fahrenheit, on his feet the whole day long.

That boy lived in miserable poverty, and it cannot be said that he enjoyed his childhood. He worked all day long, but he did not feel that he was miserable. Society at that time was much more diverse, agreeable, compassionate, and harmonious. At my advanced age of sixty-seven, I have only begun to discover the extent of the change, the destruction, and the ruin that have overtaken my country. Now no one, child or adult, can go even a quarter of a kilometer down the street alone.

That Mexican boy reminded me of my childhood and opened a door for me. I began to write the book in Mexico and finished writing it in Chicago, to serve as a living witness to a people fated to walk in bitter darkness.

the world through the eyes of **angels**

PART ONE

The Mullah

I was always overjoyed to be released from the one-room Koranic school, where children recited Koranic verses as Mullah Abdul-Hamid's long yellow bamboo whip hovered, threatening anyone who failed to repeat the verses with complete clarity. I would leave the Sheikh Mohammad Mosque next to the deep well with crumbling walls where old blind Hajj Ahmad Al-Shahdi sat. He always recognized my steps and would turn his face toward me and yell, "Don't run! Go slowly, you have time. Be careful as you cross the street." I wouldn't look at him or respond to anything he said. I would leave behind me the noise of the other children—their eyes filled with jealousy—and start to run, stopping only when I reached the other side of the street.

In those days, in 1943 and 1944, there weren't many cars in the streets. I went barefoot, winter and summer. I ran nonstop, passing through a world of beauty and delight along the way. Can I possibly describe the pleasures of that passage? Abu Shamzi's store, the summer melons, and all the shops full of beautifully colored pictures. As I ran by, I would look at the butchers' shops, the produce vendors, and the grocers. Often in the evening, poor youths would perform with the *dirbasha,* piercing their cheeks or sides with the sharp spit; and there would be music, beggars, wandering photographers, and porters with boxes full of wonders.

I would reach the center of the city, the crowded Bab Al-Toub, where the largest two streets crossed and where lavish movie posters drew my eye. I always fought the temptation to stop, by convincing myself that I would have more time to enjoy them on the way back. I often took the relatively empty street that passed through Bab Al-Saray, the large butchers' market, that took me to the Bazaar of the Seven Doors, trying my best not to be distracted by the splendors, finally entering the Atami market.

The Atami market is one of the oldest markets in Mosul, mentioned by the historian Ibn Al-Atheer. It is called the Atami market—meaning "the dark market"—because it is covered by a roof that protects it from the scorching summer sun and the drenching winter rain.

I would take the long way around in an attempt to avoid Ahmad the Mad Dog, who would either find a way to delay me, or merely hit me. I would reach my father's store out of breath. My father would smile in approval and give me his seat without saying anything.

Thinking back, more than sixty years later, I estimate it took between ten and fifteen minutes of nonstop running to get to my father's store.

Before I caught my breath, my friend Sami, the son of Hasqail, whose store was to the left of ours, would be at my side, as quick as a monkey. His father allowed him to play only with me. I was very happy to have him next to me. We would have long, engrossing conversations during which I was a model listener, living in the vast spaces that Sami's narration opened before me. I was beyond happy listening to his accounts of the many movies that he had seen and memorized. He would narrate the story and imitate its heroes, the way they stood, and the way they performed their roles.

Whenever I recall my life back then, I realize that Sami was without a doubt my guide, even though he was the same age. Our friendship began when we were five and deepened as time passed. At that age, I wasn't allowed to go to the movies. I don't know how long his stories about the movies lasted, but time passed like a flash of lightning, and my father would suddenly be there waving at us, returned from the mosque. Sami and I would leave my father's store and go to Mukhlif's store if he had no customers. Mukhlif was Jewish, like Sami, and his store was larger than Hasqail's or my father's. My father's store was stuffed with merchandise, leaving little space for me. Mukhlif would greet us with a broad affectionate smile, and give each of us a small piece of chocolate wrapped in brown paper.

Afterwards, when Sami and I were older, Sami would go with me as far as Bab Al-Toub, where we would separate, Sami returning to the market while I walked home. I walked slowly, unhurried, and the way was full of delights without end. I can see my way home still, as in a pleasant dream. I can describe some of its charms, but I can't begin to convey the profound happiness that filled me.

Most of the shops had hung on their walls pictures of all kinds that drew the eye, and at the age of five or six my greatest pleasure was the contemplation of these brightly colored images on my way home. Whenever I remember Mosul in 1943 and 1944, I am amazed by its people's love of pictures. A person who saw the pictures back then would think that he was in a cosmopolitan, international city, not in an Arab, Iraqi city. I don't know why people were so attracted to these colorful images. Was it an instinctive love of art and the wonder at it that lies so deep in us? Was it some genetic predisposition that hadn't yet been discovered? Was it the effect of the incomparable beauty of spring, which appeared in that poor, isolated city as in no other? I don't know. All I know is that the beauty of these pictures overwhelmed me to the point of numbness. They were displayed in all the shops: the butcher, the barber, the clothing store, the greengrocer, the kebab maker, the restaurant, the café, the potter, the cobbler, the smith, the perfume store, the glass store, the shoe store, and even the heel maker's store. Pictures, of many colors, that were changed and renewed constantly. The cafés, restaurants, and barbershops took greater care in choosing the pictures they displayed than other stores—especially the restaurants, whose business depended on offering customers comfort and beauty.

The wall hangings in cafés offered whoever wanted to learn about history the chance to read the artfully inscribed calligraphic paintings. Anyone entering a café would see pictures that portrayed and immortalized, with reverent comments, the Arabs since before Islam as well as the history of Iraq: Al-Muhalhil, Kuliab, Jassas, Jalilah, Antara Al-Absi casting away the enemies' heads, the Messiah Jesus and his virgin mother Mary, and Mosul's saint Mar Kourkis, who destroyed the dragon with his long lance. Ali Ben Abi Talib, Yabaris, Amrou Bin Wad Al-Amiri, Abu Nuwas, Al-Jahiz, Al-Asma'u, Sindbad, the battle of Al-Qadisiyah, Yarmouk, the massacre of Jerusalem, the crusaders' massacre of women and children, the crusaders' siege of Acre, Issa Al-Awam's swimming back and forth between the ships and Acre carrying messages in a bundle, Saladin's victories in the battle of Hateen, the historical victory over the Mongols by Qatz in Ayn Jalout, Al-Zahir Baibars, the conqueror Sultan Mohammad pounding on the doors of Constantinople, Sultan Salim rescuing the Iraqis from the bloody Safaween massacres, Hussein Pasha Al-Jalili overseeing the battle of Bash Tabiya that ended with the fall of Nader Shah, "the Napoleon of the East," the ferocious battles that had taken place hundreds of years ago between the Ottomans—with their beautiful red banner with its white crescent—and the Russians, the hated Muscovites, called *masqouf* in a derisive pun on the popular fish eaten along the river. The flowing blood of victims on either side and the cannons mired in mud. All these, along with pictures of kings and princes from all over the world, as well as pictures of the Sultan Abdel Hamid. Pictures of the grand Mohammad Ali Pasha and his relatives, and all his descendants up to and including Farouq—a never-ending list. The cafés covered their walls from top to bottom with these pictures.

The Al-Thoub Café was my favorite. There, hanging under the historical pictures, was a set of maxims in beautiful calligraphy: *Avert the malice of those to whom you have been charitable . . . Envy will not prevail . . . The height of wisdom is the fear of God . . . A kind word is like giving alms . . . There is no recompense for charity but charity . . . The eye of the envious is impaired . . . There is no God but God . . . If words are made of silver, silence is made of gold . . . Your tongue is a fortress, if you guard it, it will protect you, but if you deceive it, it will deceive you . . . He who seeks other than God's help is miserable.*

Who wouldn't enjoy contemplating a tablet bearing a beautifully inscribed verse of Al-Umari, Abu Nuwas, Al Jahiliyeen, or Al-Mu'asireen, or this one of Al-Mutanabbi's verses:

*The censure of the inadequate
is but an attestation of my completeness.*

Or this one by Abi Tamam:

*Scorn not the generous man for his open-handedness,
for water must run downhill.*

Or Abu Nuwas:

Cease blaming me, for blame is but an incitement.
Treat me with that which was itself the illness.

Or this famous verse of Al-Jahili:

Every appeal I make leaves me disappointed
Save when I call "Oh, my wealth!"

And many other poems that I can no longer recall.

There was pleasure to be found not only in the pictures and the calligraphy, but also in the astonishing skill of the craftsmen: The way the shoemaker placed the thick buffalo skin in the water and how he stretched and sewed it. How the kebab maker chopped the onions into thin rings with such precision and speed. How the jeweler transformed the long silver ingots into a thin wire a few meters long. How the carpenter pierced the wooden board with the electrical drill and inserted the bolt. Even the ironsmith drew attention with his extraordinary skill as he removed the red-hot burning iron with tongs and then flattened it by beating it with a heavy hammer, or rounded it, or turned it into a long rod and then cut it into nails to be used on horses' hooves, or for many other uses.

These were miracles to the eyes of a child who found a strange and beautiful world in the market, so alive and so different from the world of the Koranic school with "the Mullah" and his painful bamboo whip, and the endless repetition of words and sentences under the shadow of cruelty and submission, so repellent.

PART TWO

Al-Shahdi: The Refuge of the Fearful

We children disliked going to the Mullah because of the excruciating boredom of repeating the same words over and over again; but we were delighted to go and listen to the marvelous, exciting stories that Sheikh Ahmad Al-Shahdi would tell.

We had two breaks each day, and they were the happiest times that we spent at the Mullah's school. As soon as recess started, we would run like monkeys and surround the Sheikh. In good weather we would sit on the ground, but in winter we would bring one of the mats that were piled in the corner of the mosque where the roof protected the worshipers from rain.

Even Sheikh Ahmad was happy when recess started. His face would light up in a delighted smile as soon as he felt us gather around him. Thinking back, I believe the happiness he felt when we gathered around him was due to the severe isolation he lived in. His family members, who tended to him, were busy with their own affairs; the only chance he had to speak to anyone all day was when we would ask him to tell us stories. His hazel eyes, beautiful but unseeing, would brighten at the sound of gathering children, but he couldn't see any of us.

A few meters from Mullah Abdul-Hamid's door, Al-Shahdi's people had laid out for him a small, worn-out mat, which he had covered with a sheepskin on which he sat as he leaned against the wall that faced the well with the crumbling wall. Whenever it rained, and it rained a lot, he would drape the sheepskin over his head and sit unmoving. I don't know whether or not he was able to walk, but I'm certain that he never asked anyone's help in getting around. He would sit there wrapped in the sheepskin until his people would remember him and have him moved to a nearby house.

I never asked when he had lost his sight, and no one ever discussed it. All I remember is that his hearing was very good: he knew most of us as soon as we spoke, and he called us by our names. He could recognize me by the sound of the galoshes I wore; but if I was barefoot, he would ask, "Who are you?"

He was small of stature, no bigger than a small child. We never saw him standing up. The blue of the veins on the backs of his hands stood out against his white skin. His white beard was always cut and well shaped; I don't know who did that for him. The oddest memory I have of Al-Shahdi is of his sheepskin: it was full of white lice. In the winter the sun would warm his body; and so he would throw off his sheepskin, lean against the wall, and lay the skin out under the sun. The heat caused the lice to move out in all directions. The transparent bodies of the lice showed their insides full of red blood. We used to follow them and squash them, delighting in the sound when they burst under our fingernails. When I came home from the Mullah's, I would see my sister Shafaq standing there, telling me to take off my dishdasha. She would place it in the wash bin and then seat me under the faucet—when the water was warm—or bring a hot pot of water that she had prepared, and begin to wash my hair and body. She would then dress me in a clean dishdasha. She would check my head carefully for lice; that used to be the worst part of my day.

Sheikh Ahmad's stories were different from the stories our mothers told us of fabled animals like Dayou and Al Damiya. His stories were real. He told us about Sheikh Mohammad and the Sufis, about tyranny and oppression, and about travel and adventure. The best stories were the ones about the generosity of Sheikh Mohammad—who was buried there in the mosque— and the ones about the siege of Mosul. His storytelling style was supremely thrilling because he didn't talk to us like children. He always began by calling out our names, and questioning us with a respect that we never got from our parents or other adults. "Hazim, Mohammad, Ghanem, Khalil. What do you want to hear today?"

"Sheikh Mohammad and the wolves."

"And then?"

"The siege of Mosul."

"And then?"

"Stories about Abu Laila."

"I won't be able to tell you all these stories in one day."

We would all shout, "The wolves, the wolves!"

He would usually start each story with a question: "Why are winters here so severe?"

We would reply in one voice: "So that the river can freeze and the buffaloes walk on it."

We had learned that from his stories, but had never seen a buffalo walk on a frozen river and had never even seen the Tigris frozen. The only ice we had seen was on the streets of the market, where we had had many falls. The ice would look like glass and we would fall and bloody our noses and arms and return home in tears. I used to go to my sister Shafaq for comfort because she would clean my wounds, change my clothes, and send me back to the Mullah, warning me to be careful.

Though we hadn't seen any of these things, we would produce the same response, inevitably, and he would start the story in a low voice as if he were about to act out the details:

"One harsh winter the river water froze, and people and wagons and even buffaloes could move around on the ice in the daytime. The poor wolves, however, couldn't find anything to eat and almost starved to death. And so one day at dawn the guard who was opening the gate"—here the Sheikh pointed at Bab Al-Jadid, only a couple of hundred meters away—"was attacked by hundreds of wolves who devoured him in the blink of an eye, and then rushed howling through the alleys of the city, looking for more. People cowered in their homes. They stopped going to the dawn prayer and stopped going to their work."

The Sheikh stopped to ask, "What happened to the builder?"

We would all reply: "He stayed at home and never finished building."

"What happened to the butcher?"

"He stayed home and didn't go to his shop."

"What happened to the weaver?"

"The loom stopped working."

He would ask questions involving several trades, and we would reply in one voice.

In the summer Sheikh Ahmad would sit near the door in the roofed area and would point to the center of the dome and ask, "Where?"

We would all answer, "Here in your place."

He would nod in approval and say, "Yes, I sit in this place in order to receive God's blessing; that is why I have lived this long. How old am I?"

And we would all reply, "A hundred and twenty-seven years old."

"And what do you say?"
"We say may God prolong your life."
"And yours, my children."

Sheikh Mohammad *breakfasted on bread and water, and then ate one other meal for the rest of the day. Whenever people brought him more than one meal, he would give it to a needy person. There was a widow who used to bake bread every morning before dawn and deliver it to the restaurants in Bab Al-Toub, then return home to her sleeping children. On her way to the restaurant each day, she would give Sheikh Mohammad a warm loaf of bread. One day, while the widow was handing the Sheikh the bread, four wolves entered the mosque and stood at the Mullah's door. The woman let go of the bread basket and ran and took cover behind the Sheikh. The hungry wolves were staring at Sheikh Mohammad, their phosphorescent eyes gleaming and their sharp fangs bared. Sheikh Mohammad picked up four loaves of bread and threw them to the wolves. The wolves ate the bread, and then sat in front of the Sheikh happily wagging their tails. Sheikh Mohammad told the widow, "Don't be afraid, stay in the mosque till I return. He placed the basket on his head, then rose and said to the wolves, "Come, you worshipers of God."*

The wolves got up and followed him. He stopped at the entrance of every street, waiting for the wolves to catch up with him; then he threw them more bread, and went on when they were done eating. That is how he gathered a long, long line of wolves and began to walk behind them shepherding them like a herd of female sheep, all the way to Bab Al-Jadid. At the gate he stopped and said to them, "Go in peace, worshippers of God." The wolves looked at him and in one voice said, "Peace be upon you, Oh Blessed One," and the wolves left, never to return.

When Sheikh Muhammad returned to the widow, he set down the bread basket and it was full! Not a loaf was missing, and the bread was warm as if it had just been taken off the fire. He told the widow, "Go now, and trust in God."

We had heard the story many times before and knew when it would end, and so we were ready to shout, "The thief, the thief!"

One day *a policeman recognized a criminal and wanted to arrest him. The thief, who was younger than the policeman, started running away. The policeman began to shout, "Thief, thief!" People gathered and began to chase the thief. The thief had heard that Sheikh Mohammad was the protector of humans and animals in distress, so he went to the mosque and asked for Sheikh Mohammad's protection. He told the Sheikh, "I am your guest." The Sheikh said, "Roll yourself up in the mat," and the thief did. When the policeman and all the people that had followed came to the mosque, they asked the Sheikh, "Did a thief come in here?"*

The Sheikh replied, "Yes."

"Where is he?"

"Inside the mat."

The policeman told his companions, "There is no power but God's. The Sheikh has gone senile, let's go." Laughing, they all left.

A few minutes later the thief uncovered himself and angrily said to the Sheikh, "Why did you tell them where I was? Did you want them to kill me?"

The Sheikh smiled and said quietly, "Do you know what saved you?"

"No."

"My honesty. I do not lie. Truth is salvation."

For the third time, we would all shout together: "The siege, the siege!"

He would start the third story with a question: "Hazim."

"Yes."

"Are you a man?"

"Yes."

"Do you protect your family?"

"Yes."

"Would you let them be attacked by anyone?"

"No."

"Would you let the enemy kill your family?"

"No."

He would then ask all of us, "Would any of you let that happen?"

We would all shout, "No! We will never allow it!"

"We did not allow it, either. Nader Shah demanded that we open the gates of our city so that he may come in and kill us like sheep, rape our women, and then kill them along with the children. Would you have agreed to that?"

At the top of our lungs we would shout: "No, we would not agree!"

"We did not agree, either. When we heard that Nader Shah and his Persian armies were coming to attack us, the ruler Al-Hajj Hussein Al-Jalili gathered the people of Mosul outside the walls—near here—and said to them: 'Whoever wants to be killed by Nader Shah can go to him now and be killed with his family. Those who want to die honorably in battle can remain in Mosul.' We all shouted, 'Hajj Hussein, we are not cowards, we will stay and fight.'"

We the young would also shout, "Yes! We are not cowards!"

Then the Sheikh would shout, "Are you ready to die in defense of your women?"

"Yes, we are ready."

"Your pride?"

"Yes, we are ready."

"Raise your hands and follow me to death." Sheikh Ahmad would raise his thin and shaky arm and say, "All our people were ready to die. Would you have done the same, had you been with us?"

And we would all respond, "Yes, we would."

Hajj Hussein wanted to get the food and supplies ready, and so he sent people to the northern villages to buy wheat, barley, rice, lentils, cheese, fruits, and vegetables; but Nader Shah and the Persians had beaten them to it, and had attacked and pillaged the villages and their people. Our people did not have enough sustenance to maintain a long siege.

The news was spreading that Kirkuk had fallen after four days of siege, that Nader Shah had gathered all the men and killed most of them, and that he ordered his army to rape the women and then kill them and the children. The remaining men were taken prisoners and became his slaves. Irbil fell in half a day, and the same was done to its people. Nader Shah occupied all of the Kurdish and Christian villages that lay between Irbil and Zakhou, all but Mosul and a few villages. Hajj Hussein had ordered his men to mount a guard on the wall and to keep watch to the horizon in all directions. Many young men volunteered to go up on the walls to watch. A few days later the watchmen saw a black speck approaching the city from the north. They opened the gate to let him in. It was a ten-year-old boy, the only survivor of the Christian village of Batnaya. His feet were bloodied from running, and his clothes were torn by thorns. He fell unconscious as he reached the gate. They picked him up and splashed water on his face, and he woke up and began to cry. He was hungry and had wounds all over his feet and legs. They gave him food and treated his wounds, and he fell asleep, but at night he started screaming. The family that had taken him in him woke up, and he told them what he had seen happen to his village. The Persian armies came and gathered all the villagers and killed all the men, raped the women, and then killed them and the children. He had hidden in the forest. He waited for the army to leave and ran to Mosul.

Hajj Hussein ordered his people to receive all those who escaped from the Persians. When the people of Mosul heard the young boy's story, they decided to kill their women and children if Nader Shah's army occupied Mosul. My great-great-grandfather had three beautiful young girls, whom he loved very much, and one boy—my great-grandfather—who was seventeen years old. He told his son, "Omar, I cannot kill your sisters, can you?" Omar cried, and left the house.

The wise men gathered and told the people to have faith in God. "Do not kill your children; defend your city, teach the women how to fight and defend themselves and their children, and God will grant us victory."

The guns back then were very old. Each had to be loaded with gunpowder from its mouth after every shot. And so they taught everyone—men, women and children—how to use the bow and arrow. The blacksmiths and carpenters volunteered to make bows and arrows. They made thousands, and everyone was trained to use them. They divided the day into two parts: from morning till noon the women and children would train; and from noon to evening, the men would train. They all became experts at the use of the bow and arrow.

News of Nader Shah's victories continued to reach Mosul. After occupying the Kurdish and Turkmen villages, he attacked the Christian and Yazidi villages, whose people received the same brutal treatment. The few survivors escaped either to the mountains or to Mosul. The people of Mosul welcomed them all as brothers and supplied them with tents and food. The people of Mosul no longer ate by themselves in their homes: they invited the refugees to share their food and drink.

Hajj Hussein began to prepare for a long siege. People donated money and materials. Hajj Hussein asked that all should share in prayer, food, and death. He told them they were one family. When the Arabs in neighboring villages like Shamr, Al-Jabour, Abou Matyout, Al-Jaheesh, and Al-Ubaid heard about the determination of the people of Mosul, they too divided what they had and sent half of it to Mosul, and they created an army of four thousand to defend Mosul against the Persians. But Nader Shah's army surprised them, surrounded and killed them all, made off with their herds, and left their corpses to rot in the open air.

We listened, constantly worried that Mullah Abdul-Hamid would call us back to resume reciting the Koran. To keep our attention, Sheikh Ahmad would from time to time cry out to us, "Shut your eyes! Now open them again." We would close and open our eyes, and he would go on.

A split second, the time it takes to close and open one's eyes, is all it took for us to be surrounded by four hundred and fifty thousand soldiers, ten thousand or more cannons, swords, guns, bows, and all that mankind had created of weaponry. All my great-grandfather and great-great-grandfather could see as they looked out from the wall was a sea of gleaming weapons. All the plains, hills, and mountains around Mosul were covered by soldiers, as far as the eye could see, swarming like ants, as numerous as grains of sand in the desert.

Mosul was a pebble facing a raging sea, waiting to be swept away by the advancing tide. How could fifteen thousand men fight against an army of four hundred and fifty thousand?

Only fifteen thousand men knew how to use weapons; the rest were women and children. Most of the men were civilians, not professional soldiers. They did not know how to fight with swords. They had been trained, thanks to Hajj Hussein, in the use of the bow and arrow. Everyone was terrified. Women cried as they bade farewell to their husbands and sons, who awaited the end. No one could eat, or smile, or even talk. There was no escape; death surrounded us in every direction.

The Persians began to fire their cannons against specific sections of the wall and organized their troops to pierce the wall when a section collapsed, storm through the breach, and slaughter the people.

A troop of enemy soldiers headed by Nader Shah's high commander, Jayloul Khan, approached the entrance of Bab Al-Jadid.

Jayloul Khan, the leader of the Qazalbash troops, was as strong as iron. He was a giant, more than two meters tall, and his sword was more than a meter long. Riding forward on his horse, he wore red silk garments and a red silk turban with a gem that shone like the sun. He had fierce, scowling features. When he reached the wall under the gate of Bab Al-Jadid, he was only two hundred meters from us.

Sheikh Al-Shahdi would raise his gaunt arm and point to the nearby gate.

One of the Persians *shouted through a horn that magnified his voice, in Arabic: "Jayloul Khan has come to negotiate. He is the messenger of the King of Kings; the Shah of Persians and Arabs; the Alexander of the East; the conqueror of Afghanistan, China,* and India; the humbler of giants; and the destroyer of the strongest kings and princes. God protects him. Open the door and negotiate, do not be cowards."

Hajj Hussein decided to go out to the fierce-looking Jayloul and negotiate. He was warned of deception, but he said, "Who am I? Let them kill me. I am one of you—if they kill me, choose another to take my place."

Before he had finished talking, the gate was opened and he rode out alone on his Arabian horse. He carried no weapon. A group of young swordsmen followed him, carrying only their swords.

Standing in front of Jayloul Khan, he looked like a gazelle before an elephant. Jayloul Khan was surprised at the speed of his response, and said to him through a translator, "Why aren't you carrying your weapons?"

Hajj Hussein smiled and said, "I heard you say you wanted to negotiate. Negotiators need no weapons."

Jayloul Khan said, "That's correct. You are wise. Why don't you make the wise decision and spare Muslim blood?"

"It is you who should protect Muslim blood. We are defending ourselves and our honor. If you wish to spare Muslim blood, leave us to live peacefully in our countries, and live as you wish in yours."

"You are infidels and must obey us."

"Just now you said that we should spare Muslim blood, and now you call us infidels?"

"We are the Muslims, not you, and we will not allow infidels to kill even one of us. Not even one. One of us equals a nation of infidels."

Hajj Hussein smiled and said, "Only God knows who of us is the infidel."

Sheikh Al-Shahdi would stop at this point and shout, "Are we infidels?"

"No, we are Muslims, we read the Koran!"

"Why then did they want to kill us? Do you accept that?"

And we would all respond, "No!"

Jayloul Khan said, "Open the doors then, and we will offer you security, and only kill the Jews, Christians, and Yazidis."

Hajj Hussein replied, "Everyone here is under our protection. We are all brothers. We have lived together, and so did our parents and grandparents, and so will our children. We will not surrender any of them."

Sheikh Ahmad would shout, "Will you surrender your brothers to the enemy?"

And we would all respond, "No, my brother is like me!"

The giant Jayloul then said, "If the gates are not opened we will attack you tomorrow. Fair warning."

Hajj Hussein smiled and said, "We will not open the gates, do as you please."

Hajj Hussein returned, and the gate of Bab Al-Jadid was closed. After the dawn prayer hundreds of cannons began to fire on the walls and the city. This went on for eight days, and many refugees whose tents were near the wall were killed. Hajj Hussein sent the refugee women and children to live in houses, while the Muslim and Yazidi men lived in the mosques, the Christians in churches, and the Jews in synagogues. Hundreds of houses were destroyed; the earth was set on fire and the air was filled with smoke. It became difficult to see through the thickness of the dust and smoke.

In spite of all that, the people organized themselves into fire brigades, rebuilt homes, and treated the wounded. But dozens of bombs were falling every minute and people were overcome with desperation and despair. On the eighth day, they were exhausted and seemed close to preferring death to the suffering they had endured. Suddenly the religious and the Sufis and the mystic men spread throughout the city, loudly praying and asking God: "Lord, darkness has fallen on us and left us weak, where is our escape?"

Thousands of women, children, and elderly Muslims, Christians, Jews, and Yazidis joined in the prayer, shouting: "Allah, Allah, Allah lives."

"Allah, Allah, Allah lives."

"Lord, darkness has fallen on us and left us weak, where is our escape?"

"Allah, Allah, Allah lives."

Bands of musicians accompanied the invocations and prayers. The fighters regained their energy and will to fight, at which point Hajj Abdul Fatah, brother to Hajj Hussein, shouted: "Who will pledge martyrdom with me?"

All the youths came out; one of them my great-grandfather, who was seventeen. The Hajj told them, "Go and bid your families farewell, for none of us will return."

When my great-grandfather arrived home, his mother and sisters hugged him and his father asked, "Why did you volunteer? You are our only son."

He replied, "I will not see my mother and sisters killed. I will die before I let that happen."

He then joined the Feda'yeen, the martyrs. Hajj Hussein asked them to wear their shields and armor, but they said, "We are martyrs! We will wear nothing but our coffins. We want to be light, to move and strike fast." When the enemy saw them riding out from the gate, their champions came forward, Jayloul Khan the Giant at their head. He was waving his sword, foaming at the mouth, and

promising death to anyone who approached him. He was capable of
slicing a horseman in two with one stroke. Instinctively and with
the fervor of one who wants to die, my great-grandfather launched
himself on his horse toward the enemy and hurled his spear at Jay-
loul Khan from a distance of ten meters. The spear flew through
the air, and Jayloul could not believe his eyes. He tried to catch it,
but the spear swerved and struck his neck and he fell off his horse,
swimming in blood, while the Feda'yeen cheered: "Allahu akbar!"

The Feda'yeen drove into Nader Shah's army as a knife cuts
into a piece of meat. The exhortations of the besieged city reached
them and strengthened their yearning for death. "Lord, darkness
has fallen on us and left us weak, where is our escape?"

"Allah, Allah, Allah lives; Allah, Allah, Allah lives."

When they realized that the enemy was trying to encircle them
from behind, they withdrew to the city, and Hajj Hussein opened
the gate. They had killed more than a hundred and fifty enemy sol-
diers, along with their leader Jayloul. Thirty Feda'yeen were killed.

The people regained their courage, and were cheering wildly.
Nader Shah wanted to break their will, so he ordered his soldiers to
cut up the bodies of the dead Feda'yeen and have them thrown to
the dogs.

The story of the siege of Mosul was endless. The Sheikh knew
each and every detail. How many of its people were killed under
the bombardment. How many Christians, Jews, Yazidis, and
refugees. How many of Nader Shah's soldiers had been killed.
How the Shah had lost and retreated with his mighty and
defeated army, seen off by the cheers and songs of the city that
had shaken the earth beneath the strongest army in the world.
How more than ten thousand soldiers from the Shah's army

had been killed. How this small and poor city had become the miracle of the ages.

Sheikh Al-Shahdi would shout with all his strength: "What is the most honorable of cities?"

Clapping, we would all reply: "Mosul!"

"What is the most courageous of cities?"

"Mosul!"

"Which one? Which one?" And he would go on with the story: *The people of Mosul went out into the streets, singing, dancing, and celebrating. They beat the drums and began to rebuild the wall, fearing a surprise return of the Persians. Hajj Hussein rebuilt all the homes at his own expense.*

How old was Sheikh Ahmad? No one knew. When we asked him he would say one hundred and twenty-seven years. He would add a year to his age every Eid, because, according to him, he was born in the early days of the Eid. Of course he used the Muslim *Hijra* calendar, which has six days less than the Western calendar. No one ever told me his real age.

Mullah Abdul-Hamid doubted Al-Shahdi's memory; he would say he was older than he admitted by at least ten to twenty years. Mullah Abdul-Hamid said Al-Shahdi had been a hundred and twenty-seven years old when he met him more than twenty years earlier.

I can never recall the Sheikh Mohammad Mosque without Al-Shahdi. He was like the dome, the Mullah's room, like the deep well. A permanent fixture all fall, winter, and spring—though he disappeared every June and returned in August.

I don't know how Al-Shahdi's life ended. I forgot all about him when I started school and had so many other doors opened to me through reading. I had heard nothing more of him when

I moved in 1954 to Baghdad to complete my studies. That meant he was still alive, for if he had died I would have heard and insisted on being one of the pallbearers at his funeral. I had still heard nothing about Al-Shahdi's death when I returned to Mosul in 1956 for my father's funeral.

PART THREE

Miss Khadija and the Carrot

The first day at school was the most important day of my life because that was the day I began to uncover the secrets of great pictures. On that day I was able to compound my pleasure by learning the names of all the great historical figures immortalized in the pictures. This one is Antara, and that one is Abu Zayd Al-Hilali, that one is King Farouq, and this one is George the Sixth, and that one the Shah of Iran, and here is the Conqueror Mohammad, and on and on. Before that day I used to enjoy just looking at the pictures and colors, but now I learned the name of each individual in the pictures.

From that day on I was a man in full. The butcher gave me a piece of liver, just for me. And that summer my father assigned me a disagreeable task, but one that had its enjoyable aspects: he asked me to sell hats and fans in the restaurants and markets.

I had accompanied some of my cousins in this chore during holidays. But now I had become an unwanted competitor. They were a couple of years older and were good salesmen. They used to earn one fils for each item they sold. I, however, was not paid, because the merchandise was my father's—and that was the disagreeable part. The enjoyment came from having the door opened to the delight of reading the enchanting calligraphy that filled the cafés and shops and markets. It was the beginning of my learning about all these great people and families, a pleasure that money itself could not buy.

It was, however, a hard-earned pleasure. When I was six years old, the Al-Ahdath school refused to register me. It was a mixed school for boys and girls only a couple of hundred paces from my home. I went with my mother to register. I was barefoot and wearing a dishdasha. I returned home distressed at being refused and very anxious to go to school. I didn't know why I had been rejected. My registration was delayed for a few days until my father bought me a pair of gray trousers, a white shirt, and some shoes.

I was very happy to have my first pair of shoes. In the summer I used to go barefoot; in winter or when the temperature dropped to the freezing point, my father would buy me a pair of cheap and simple galoshes made of leather covered with a layer of cloth. The galoshes were enough because I never had to walk too far. My daily trips were to the nearby Sheikh Mohammad Mosque for the Koranic sessions, and then to the market at noon to allow my father to perform his prayers. Later on I had to buy things for breakfast from Bab Al-Jadid, and deliver Sabika's dinner tray.

The shoes had a strange and repulsive smell, but to me—at the time—they smelled not only natural but pleasant. When I went to bed at night, I placed them next to my pillow and felt great pleasure at seeing them there in the morning. I got dressed and was very anxious to put them on. When my sister Shafaq saw what I had done, she started to laugh and called everyone to come and see.

I had put the shoes on the wrong feet. Shafaq, while laughing, helped me put them on the right feet and tied the laces, leaving several holes unstrung, which again made everyone laugh.

I was very anxious to get to school. On the way, I kept pulling on my mother's cloak, trying to make her go faster. She pulled back, fearing that her head would be uncovered, and yelled at me to leave it alone. She insisted that I let go of her cloak and shouted at me, "Leave me alone! Walk ahead of me."

I began to run and almost fell. It was the first time I had ever worn anything heavy on my feet. The shoes made me feel as if there was a smooth, slippery separation between me and the ground. I slowed down in fear of falling or getting my expensive new clothes dirty. I was very proud of my new clothes.

When I arrived at Al-Ahdath, I saw that there were others wearing much better clothes. On the first day of school I became acquainted with Ghanem, the second best friend, after Sami, that I have ever had. We were the same age. His shirt, sewn by his mother, was better-looking and very colorful. I didn't care. The important thing was that I was registered at school. I was very anxious to go to class when the bell rang. I ran and almost fell again, so I slowed down.

When the young blond teacher Miss Khadija saw me, she smiled, patted my head, and said, "Now you're OK." She had been there when my mother brought me to school the first time, when I was rejected for wearing a dishdasha and being barefoot. She asked a tall student who was sitting at the front of the class to move back and give me his seat. She then gave us the reading book *Al Khaldouniya,* a book full of beautiful colored pictures: a water jug, a barrel, a broom, a pencil, a chalkboard, and so on. First she told us to look at the blackboard where she had written the alphabet. She would point and say the name of the letter, and we would loudly repeat after her: *alif, ba, ta,* and so on. She then asked us to open the book to the first page, and the teaching began.

I don't know what happened to me: as soon as I opened the first page I began—for the first time in my life—to actually read, and in five minutes I had finished reading the whole book. I didn't know that Miss Khadija was watching me.

I was seated at the front of the class. To my right there was a girl whose features and name I have forgotten, but I remember she had a dark complexion and was very thin. Miss Khadija came up to me and said angrily, "Why are you playing? Learn how to read first. Here we don't just look at the pictures—you can look at the pictures when you get home."

My dark-skinned neighbor began to cry. I don't know why. Maybe she got scared when she saw the teacher angrily swoop down on me, or perhaps she thought we would both be punished. I was upset, too, but got hold of myself and said, "I *am* reading, not playing."

The teacher said, "If you pay attention, you'll learn how to read."

I mustered my courage and said, "I know how to read."

With a challenging look she pointed to the book and said, "Fine. Read."

"Where?"

"The first page."

I opened the first page and read several pages in a minute. Each page had one or two words. At that point she stopped frowning and smiled. She patted my head and said, "Are you repeating the class?"

"No."

"How is it you know how to read?"

"I finished the Koran at the Mullah's."

"Can you write?"

"I haven't written before, but I think I can write now."

She laughed and asked me to go to the blackboard and write my name.

I went to the blackboard and wrote my name, my father's and grandfather's names, and everything else she asked me to write.

At the beginning of the second class, Miss Khadija came with Miss Kawakib, the school principal. The principal was also blond and elegant, but always frowning, never smiling. The teacher pointed to me. I got up, and she said, "Write on the blackboard, 'I am a good student.'" And I did. She then asked me to write another sentence, and after I did that she asked if I knew how to write numbers, and told me to write whatever five numbers I knew. I wrote up to ten and was asked to stop. Miss Khadija said, as she looked at the principal with a smile, "He deserves to be registered in the third grade, not the first or second. He reads better than a sixth-grader."

The principal answered while patting my head, "We can't do that. The registration period is over. If only he had come three days earlier." I recalled the argument that had taken place at home between my mother and my brother Ahmad the Mad Dog. My mother had begged him to register me, but he refused, shouting, "I've told you fifty times, school is useless! He'll leave school like I did, as soon as he fails the middle school test. Send him to the store. I know how to teach him. I'll use the whip." At the time, I didn't know what they were arguing about. I was content at the Mullah's and feared the Mad Dog, so when he left, I begged her not to send me to him.

When Miss Kawakib left, the teacher smiled, patted my head, and said, "I'm sorry." I didn't realize back then why she had apologized. What was the difference? I was happy not to have gone to work for the Mad Dog. At least no one at school beat me for no reason.

To this day I don't know why I had suddenly—and specifically on that day—known how to read. I remember an incident that occurred during the summer, about a month before registering at school. It was my first and last failed attempt to read from a book other than the Koran. I remember being at the Koranic school with the Mullah reading the Koran. I don't think I had memorized it, and I know I couldn't read the words in the middle of a sura, a Koranic verse. I knew how to read the beginning of each sura—the colors and artwork of each one were imprinted in my mind. But to read a word within a sura, I had to restart the verse from the beginning and follow it through. I still don't understand why that was; I've often wondered about it. My mother says I was sent to the Mullah before I had turned three, perhaps at two and a half, because the Sheikh Mohammad Mosque was very close to our house. She says my father asked the Mullah not to hit me, and asked him to let me just listen until I turned four. I stayed there till I was six. Three years of listening and seeing the Koran must have been imprinted in my mind, and this enabled me to read in a sort of global way. But I can't be certain.

That summer one of the Mad Dog's friends placed in front of me a copy of *Al Mukhtar* magazine, put out by *Reader's Digest*, and asked me to read the title. I couldn't. He said, "How can you read the whole Koran without being able to read a single word from this magazine?" I was embarrassed; I knew he was right, but had no answer. He pointed to the letter *alif,* and asked, "What's this?"

"Alif."

"What's this?"

"Lam." He asked me to name all the letters in the title, and I knew them all. He then asked me to say the whole word, and after several tries, I said *"al muhtar."*

He laughed. "It's *al mukhtar,* not *al muhtar.*" After that, I would only read the Koran—and then the first day of school came. I read the whole book of *Al Khaldouniya* during the first hour of the first day of class. Miss Khadija patted my head and smiled at me and kept repeating, "Excellent! Good! Bravo!"

I felt proud because she looked at me with pride and amazement. She assigned me to help teach other students while she was busy. At the end of the fourth lesson she told me that she lived in Bab Al-Iraq, described her house, and asked if I could pick up her lunch. Her house was close to the Al-Radwani Mosque, perhaps a few hundred meters from my house. Sometimes I used to accompany my father to the Al-Radwani Mosque, so I nodded yes.

"Go now."

I followed her directions. I knocked on the door and her mother answered. She looked a lot like Miss Khadija, with the exception of a few white hairs that had stolen into her yellowish braid. She asked my name, and then asked me to sit on a bamboo chair.

I sat down while she poured the rice, broth, and fresh vegetables into separate containers and placed them in the tiffin-box. She handed me a peeled orange carrot, kissed my forehead, and said goodbye. I returned to school before the end of the fourth-period lesson, and so Miss Khadija patted my head and said, "Bravo, you did well. Where would you go if I let you leave before the end of the school day?"

I thought instantly of the wonders that I encountered on my way home from the market. "I would run to my father's store and give him a chance to go to noon prayers."

She smiled and said, "I'll let you go, but on one condition."

"What is it?"

"You have to be careful crossing the street."

I nodded, smiling. "I promise."

PART FOUR

Selam

"Run, before the prayer call whisks your father away."

As soon as Mullah Abdul-Hamid uttered these words, I would jump up and start to run. I hardly stopped for a moment, whether before or after I was enrolled in school, or whether during the school year or in summer vacation. I ran barefoot, never stopping, like the weaver's shuttle.

Ahmad the Mad Dog never let me rest for an instant. The mere sight of me resting set him off. And yet, strangely, his violent oppression—which fell on me when I was a child of five and continued until adolescence—granted me entry into vast new worlds that enriched my spirit and will stay with me to the end of my days.

My bare feet, running, and the black burning street in the summer are all linked to my first cherished memory: Selam. They settled in the depths of me and became a part of me. The asphalt burned the bottoms of my feet. It forced me to stick to the walls, seeking the shade. And without being aware of it, I started to automatically walk near walls, without thinking about it, summer and winter, whether the weather was hot or cold. Years later, my wife's colleagues from work noticed that and teased her: your husband slinks along hugging the walls.

"You want some water?"

I was startled. A girl about the same age as me, maybe nine years old. Very thin. Clear of skin, wide-eyed. Barefoot like me. A smile that emanated coolness and ease in that overheated air. Panting, I had stopped. My mouth was dry. The narrow alley had offered a little shade, which was hard to come by at that hour on a burning summer day, devoid of any moisture, in our city of stone.

"Come."

She took me by the hand and pulled me along gently, smiling and looking me in the eye. I had almost passed out from the fatigue and thirst. A dusty alley, not very long, a little crooked. It was unpaved, a dead end giving access to three houses. I passed by it every day, but I had never looked into it. The first door on the left was open. She went in before me, leading me. The wooden door was ancient, without any lock, opening to the left. There was a stout piece of wood leaning against the wall. I had seen others like it in old houses: it was used to bar the door, shoved through two hasps, one on the door and the other on the wall. Now when I remember that old door, it occurs to me that it might have been the oldest door of its kind that remained in Mosul, and the most primitive.

We went along a dark passage that sloped down gently to a packed-earth courtyard that was swept clean and sprinkled with water, about five meters long by six wide, with a well in the middle. It was shaded by a mulberry tree growing in the yard of the neighboring house, standing beyond a solid wall, a few meters high, built of stone and plaster. At the back of the yard was a room with the door standing open. Stretched out in the opening was a young woman, perhaps twenty-five years old. Her features bore a strong resemblance to the little girl's. This woman was pale and gaunt, mere skin and bones. It almost looked as if her clear white skin had disappeared, leaving only the bones visible. She opened her eyes as soon as she heard us come in. A spark of happiness shone for an instant in her large, beautiful eyes, and then she closed them again. I sensed that she was very ill. That was the first time in my life that I had seen a person so ill and so disturbingly emaciated. Her coal-black hair flowed over the ends of the pillow, almost reaching the mat on which she lay. In the intense heat, sweat covered her face in an oily sheen.

Nodding as if she had known me for ages, the little girl said in a tender voice, "You're thirsty, aren't you?" Before I could answer, she let go of my hand and went toward the well. This well was different from the one in the courtyard at the Sheikh Muhammad Mosque. The well at the mosque was enclosed by a dilapidated wall, and its pail was made of leather. The only time I saw Mullah Abdul-Hamid use it was when the water from the tap was cut off. That was also in summer, as I recall. The mullah pulled up two buckets full of water and emptied them onto the floor of the small courtyard hoping to cool it. It was impossible for us children to pull the big heavy bucket up out of the well. We would approach the crumbling wall cautiously, above all being careful not to lean on it for fear it would collapse and we would fall into the well. The only time I went close and looked down into it, I saw at a great depth a small circular piece of blue sky, like a mirror with uneven edges. Later we learned to toss in small pebbles and wait a moment for the sound as they plopped into the water. We used to have great fun with that, but the mullah's stick was waiting for us whenever he saw one of us throw in a pebble, and eventually we stopped playing with the well.

The well in the little girl's courtyard was solidly built. A child could lean on it and look down into the well without being afraid of falling. It wasn't deep, perhaps only three meters. I looked around the courtyard and saw that it had no water tap like the one at our house, and I realized that the girl and her mother must drink from the well. My companion stood near the well. She said, "Wait." Then she began to pull on a rope that creaked as it slid over a piece of leather nailed to the cross-beam fixed on two tall posts on either side of the well. I looked down at the bottom, but, because the water was in movement, I didn't see the sky as I had in the well at the Sheikh Muhammad Mosque. It looked more like broken glass, fleeting and unstable. I wondered how a girl that skinny could pull up a big heavy bucket so nimbly. But then I saw a small clay jug emerge instead of a leather pail.

I had drunk river water once and was struck by the strong, rank smell of fish, and I expected the well water to have the same repellent smell. The girl took the jug and offered it to me, nodding her pretty head, her two braids flopping on her chest. "Drink."

When she saw me hesitating, she set the jug on the rim of the well and ran into the room, bringing back a small aluminum cup. She poured the water into it and offered it to me. The water was cool and tasty, with a sort of light bitterness that was not unpleasant. I drank the whole cup. She started to laugh. The water made my body break out in a sweat in the intense heat. She filled the cup again and offered it to me. I drank some of it, and then returned it to her. She took it to her mother.

There was a white rag on the mat. She soaked it in water and began to wipe her mother's forehead, face, and neck. Mother and daughter were both wearing old faded robes with necklines descending almost to the breasts, made of what we called *sheet*, using the English word for the cheap printed cloth the drapers sold in the market for women's clothing. The girl began to sprinkle what remained of the water on her mother's body. Her mother smiled with a sweet thankfulness but said nothing, perhaps because speaking required an effort she could not muster. But her eyes shone with unmistakable happiness. Then the girl went and filled the cup again and returned to her mother. She raised her head and began to give her water, holding the cup to her lips. After that the girl poured herself some and drank and then threw the jug back into the well. She took me by the hand and led me to a piece of cardboard on the ground near the wall, shaded by the mulberry tree. She said, "Sit down."

I sat. She went into the room and brought out an aluminum plate containing some washed mulberries. The berries had fallen from the tree onto the unpaved, moistened ground of the courtyard, and she had gathered them and washed them on the rim of the well. She sat near me on the cardboard and smiled. "Eat."

She pointed at the berries. They were white, very large, and delicious. But there were only a few of them. I hesitated. I took one and put it in my mouth. Suddenly my cheek was warm. This I had not expected at all: she kissed me, smiling. "Eat."

The intimacy astonished me. Embarrassment overwhelmed me. My mother always said that when I was embarrassed my ears turned as red as beets; I could not see my ears, but I felt them burning. I began to chew the berry. She did not eat. I stopped eating, too, after that first berry.

Then I remembered my errand: to bring home the sewn garments from Umm Ghanem, my friend Ghanem's mother. I had taken them to her the day before so she could sew them for the Mad Dog.

The Mad Dog sold cloth to the poor Arab peasants, and he sent the cut pieces to Mary the Christian so that she, her sister "Madeleine the Beautiful," and her mother could sew them into garments. Mary's house was in the Meidan quarter, near the old

Atami market. It took only five minutes to get there running. When more peasants came, the Mad Dog ordered me to take them to Umm Ghanem. Her house was somewhat far away, in the Talami district—farther away than our house—and it took me about fifteen minutes—running without stopping in the merciless summer heat—to get there.

The Mad Dog used to hit me for the most trivial reasons, or without any reason at all, and with extraordinary cruelty. As soon as I remembered that I was late, I jumped up and cried out to the girl, "I'll be back tomorrow." Then I shot away, oblivious.

Umm Ghanem, however, delayed me by a few more minutes, as she was putting the final touches on a dress for one of the peasant women.

As it happened, things turned out all right, and for once the Mad Dog didn't mistreat me. But I kept thinking about the little girl. Her striking beauty, her smile, her fineness, her warm kiss on my cheek, the whiteness of both her and her mother's clear skin, the jet-blackness of their hair, were all extraordinary. I never saw anything like them in my life until I traveled outside of Iraq for the first time fifteen years later and was deposited by an airplane at the Paris airport. It so happened that a Korean or Japanese airplane—I'm not sure which—was disgorging its crew of stewardesses, a bouquet of females of tremendous beauty. They drew my eye and the eye of everyone they passed with the whiteness of their pure limpid skin and the blackness of their ebony hair. Then I remembered Selam and her mother, her kiss, and the well and the mulberry tree.

In my father's shop there was an unused rope, carefully coiled. I grabbed it the next morning. In the courtyard of the shop I gathered some large sheets of paper. These had been used to wrap bales of cloth and had been discarded there by my friend

Hamu the porter because he could not sell them or use them for anything. And as I thought that the Mad Dog might send me that afternoon to bring back another batch of sewn garments from Umm Ghanem, I took the papers and the rope with me from my father's. And just as I expected, the Mad Dog dispatched me on another mission to Umm Ghanem.

As I hurried along with the rope and the papers, I picked up a stone from the street and put it in my pocket. Selam was waiting for me at the mouth of the alley, as if she had known when I was coming. Her joy was boundless when she saw me! She rushed to embrace me, and my cheek burned with another of her exquisite kisses. She took me by the hand and pulled me into the house, saying, "I thought you weren't coming." And I realized that she had been waiting for a long time. She squeezed my hand tightly as if she were afraid I might escape her. As soon as we got into the small house she cried, "*Yumma!* He's here! *Yumma!* He's here!" I saw a wide smile on her mother's face, but she did not open her eyes. And just as on the day before, she didn't say a word. I realized that the girl was telling her mother about me.

I took the stone out of my pocket and tied one end of the rope around it. She watched me and asked, "What's that? Why are you doing that?" Then I spread the large sheets of paper beneath the branches of the mulberry tree, and tossed the stone up so that the rope wound around one of the branches. I shook the branch with the rope and a thick shower of berries fell, filling the papers completely. The little girl began to laugh gleefully and wholeheartedly as she gathered up the berries. Then she washed them in cool water from the well. We sat in the shade, which did little to abate the intense heat. We began to eat the berries, with great delight. We sat touching each other, and the sweat of our bodies soaked our clothes and made us stick together. In

weather like that, touching another person's body can be a tor-
ment, pushing people apart, but despite the external heat I felt
as cool as ice inside. It was as if her body were an extension of
mine; it was as if I were in an equilibrium in which the interior
overpowered all exterior existence.

From repeated visits I learned that her name was Selam. It
was a strange name. Selma, Saalima, and Salima were common.
She might have been nicknamed Selloum, or Suleima. But I had
never in my life met anyone named Selam, either before then
or since. I fell in love with the name for the beautiful way it fell
on the ear. The time I spent with Selam was time stolen from
paradise. My happiness was supreme, especially after she showed
me how to roll marbles all the way down from the ancient door
of their house to make a complete circuit of the well and come
to rest in a hole near it. She had dug a long passage for this purpose. If she placed a marble at the highest point of this path, it
rolled continuously on a long journey which traversed almost ten
meters. She had two dark-green marbles, and we would put them
at the starting point and walk along with them laughing as they
rolled on their long way. Our delight peaked when the second
ran into the first and produced a wonderful musical tone that
made us clap.

One day I wanted to surprise her. Moshe and Sasson and
Haroun were three so-called "Uzbek" Jews who sold children's
toys. In Mosul, *Uzbek* means a seller of fake jewelry, silver and
plastic bangles, and other trinkets. I remembered that they had
some really beautiful marbles of different sizes. My daily wages
were only five fils. With that I bought from Haroun one big marble and four small ones in brilliant colors of great beauty. They
cost six fils. When I told him I would bring him the one fils the

next day, he said, "That's all right, you can owe me." Perhaps he did that out of mere neighborliness. Or perhaps out of gratitude because he had more than once asked me to bring him water in the pitcher from Al-Aghwat Mosque. Haroun put the marbles in a little brown paper bag and said, good-naturedly but with just a hint of reproach, "You're too smart to play with fisheyes." That's what we called marbles.

I was embarrassed, and I couldn't look him in the eye. I didn't try to defend myself. He was right. If not for Selam, I would never have played with them again, to the day I died. I took off running. I hid the marbles at my father's, because Ahmad the Mad Dog would have beaten me if he had seen me with them. He might have believed they distracted me from his endless demands.

What joy seized Selam when she saw the brilliant marbles! She hugged me. My cheek burned with more than one kiss. We began to roll the smaller marbles together from near the door, and then we rolled the big one after them. I don't know why, but it rolled faster than the others. Sometimes it leapt over them and hopped out of the path, making us laugh.

The next day I spent my wages on five pieces of colored candy from Bab al-Serai, and when I offered them to Selam she couldn't comprehend what was happening. She rushed over to her mother, crying out with great delight, "*Yumma, Yumma, Yumma,* look!" She squatted by her mother, telling her loudly what had happened. She repeated it several times, and her mother smiled happily. Then Selam pulled me to our place under the branches of the mulberry tree. We sat on the cardboard. She threw her slender arm around my neck. She put her head on my chest for a moment and sighed with contentment. Then she raised her head. She turned to me, looked me in the eye, and took a piece of candy. She stared at it for a moment and a smile filled her beautiful, clear face. I wondered if she had ever eaten candy before. Instead of putting the candy in her mouth, she stuck out her sharp little red tongue and licked it. Then she laughed. "It's so good!" She tasted it again and laughed, then broke it into two pieces with her teeth. She offered me half of it; and when I refused, she burned my cheek with her sweet, warm lips. She opened the little bag. She said, "Two for you and two for me."

I refused, saying, "They're all for you." When she said it again, I threatened to leave.

"Don't leave." She agreed to take the candy. Then she stared at me. To this day I remember those extraordinary deep black eyes, as she opened them wide with that elemental, unpracticed charm. She stood up quickly with a mischievous energy. "I'll show you something," she said. There was an empty cooking oil tin nearby. She brought it over and put it near the wall that was exposed to the burning sun, opposite the mulberry tree wall. The wall was high, built of stone and plaster. With the passage of time, the plaster had aged and cracked from the rains and from wear and tear, and now there were large crevices in it, which had been deepened by the sparrows and packs of lizards making their nests and burrows. Selam climbed onto the tin, reached into a hole in the wall, and pulled out something wrapped in a scrap of brown cloth. She unwrapped it with reverent movements and eagerly beckoned to me. "Look."

There were five marvelously colored pebbles: greenish yellow, glittering coal black, red, yellow-streaked, and bright green.

"Aren't they amazing?"

"Yes."

I went to the river every day in the summer to soak the baskets, fans, and brooms for my father's shop in the refreshing, cleansing water, because articles made of palm fronds dry and crack in hot weather unless soaked in water. Often I saw colored stones like those, but I didn't have the artistic gift to pick up the beautiful ones and save them.

"I got them at the beach when I was little."

I will always reproach myself for my stupidity and my lack of consideration. I didn't ask her then whom she had gone to the beach with. If only I had, I would have learned a few things about her, and perhaps I could have helped her later on. It was mere obtuseness.

She said, "Take them."

I refused. She insisted in vain. Maybe she did that in reaction to my bringing her the fisheyes or the pieces of candy. But I convinced her that the Mad Dog would kill me if he saw me with them. She finally gave in. She climbed up on the hot tin again and put her treasure back in its hiding place. If I had searched for an entire year by myself, I would not have been able to find the hole in which Selam hid her beautiful stones, as it was a long way from the steps that led to the roof.

When she got down off the oil tin, her robe, which was very old and a little bit too tight, split all the way up to her right hip, and her skin appeared, whiter and purer than her bewitching face. Her eyes clouded and I thought she was going to cry. But she mastered herself and forced a smile. She put her hand over her hip to cover her nakedness and said, "I'll sew it up. I have a needle and thread."

I felt bad. When I remember it now, I think she had probably been wearing the same dress for more than two years and that she was the one who took care of herself and her mother.

I can't remember what we talked about, but I spent almost half an hour with her. I learned that she didn't go to school at all.

It didn't occur to me to ask why, and she didn't say. But I remember that she said she wished she could go, and that she saw the little children hurrying to school in the morning, books in hand, and wished she were going with them. I volunteered to teach her to read and write. She jumped on me and made my cheek burn with more kisses.

I came back the following day. From a long way off I saw her standing there waiting for me, and the sun had almost roasted her. I had brought with me my arithmetic notebook from the past school year. I chose it because I had only used half of it. I also had a pencil and a sharpener and an eraser. Selam had filled the plate with berries, washed them, and put a piece of paper over them so the flies couldn't get to them. When we took our places on the cardboard, she put the plate in front of me and sat cross-legged, ready to pay attention to my teaching. Then she did exactly as I told her. She learned fast, and on the first day she was able to write a few words, including my name and hers, and *well, door, mat, face, tree, berry,* and *rope.* I imagine she was helped in her fast learning by a good measure of innate intelligence, as well as her age, which was about the same as mine. I also noticed that she had sewn up her dress, and it appeared even tighter on her extremely thin body.

I was surprised on the following day when she hurried to show me the notebook before we sat down, her cheeks glowing with joy. She opened it and I saw that she had copied the words that I had told her to copy ten times, and in a very beautiful hand. She said, "Close your eyes." I obeyed her and closed my eyes.

"Open them."

I opened them. A page of the notebook was before my eyes, and on it was something that startled me. There was a drawing of her mother, sleeping on the mat, framed by her wonderful ebony hair. Then on another page was a drawing, from memory, of me shaking the branch of the mulberry tree with the rope. Her pleasure at accomplishing this miracle was profound. And the drawings deserved praise and wonder. She had a gift that was years ahead of her age. Her mother's fine features were very clear. As for mine, they weren't like that, except for my nose. And yet it was a picture of me. Anyone could identify me by looking at it. Astounded, I exclaimed, "You're a genius."

She asked, "What's a genius?"

I couldn't find a synonym. I simply said, "It means smart."

She smiled and gave me a quick kiss. Then she drew me to our place in the shade of the mulberry tree.

She sat touching me. She leaned her head on mine. She whispered, "Close your eyes and try to see me. Then you'll be able to draw me like I drew you."

I closed my eyes, trying to picture her. But I didn't know what was happening to me. How does a child deal with feelings that cast him into distant worlds, where there is nothing but his dissolution into atoms that float happily, without knowing how he got there? Feelings that drag him into the depths of an abyss in a magnificent sea that whirls him around endlessly? Her features before me were bathed in a revivifying translucent light, as in deep green cold waters. We were floating, holding hands, coming up to the surface of the water, then diving again. We were surrounded by millions of fish and other living things, calm and benign, there to protect us from predators. We stood atop a high mountain, enveloped in clouds, and then fell together, our hands clasped. We saw the yawning abyss, and we thought we would fall into it and die; but then we saw ourselves on the crest of a wave that cast us into green virgin forests, and we came to rest in the highest branches of giant trees. We stretched out our hands, which became beating wings, so that we could plunge again into the depths of the water, and saw water nymphs who seized us by the hands, and we all began to dance together with unflagging vigor, and we danced until we lost consciousness.

How long I was lost in that dream, as if suspended in a pot of honey, I don't know. I remember that I dozed off and then was startled awake by the image of the Mad Dog threatening me. I jumped up hurriedly. She too was startled from her doze. I said, "I have to go." I hurried away. And when I turned at the mouth of the alley I saw her waving at me, standing near the door, smiling her forced smile, her eyes clouded with tears.

The *Eid al-Kebir*—"the Great Feast"—was imminent, and with the season Ahmad the Mad Dog saw his poor peasant customers increase in number. Most of them were from the Sharqat region and Qayara, and they came to the market only once a year, after the harvest. They came in droves after finishing the harvest to buy clothes for themselves and their families, and with their swelling numbers came an increase in my mileage. The pieces of the garments that they bought had to be sewn; and the houses of the seamstresses that did the job lay in the northern and southern parts of the city. And there was no way to transport them other than me, barefoot and bareheaded under the sun, in a temperature that even in the shade was fifty degrees Centigrade, or around 120 degrees Fahrenheit. The black asphalt of the street burned the soles of my feet. I ran until I almost passed out from thirst and dehydration. Often my nose bled, staining my white dishdasha, and I would run to the nearest water tap and put my head under it to cool off. If I was late, the Mad Dog would slap my face, and my nose would bleed again. But I learned from the Mad Dog to resist and endure. My supreme goal was not to let him see me cry. I refused to cry when his blows rained down on my face, increasing in fury and not stopping until my nose bled onto my clothes or one of the neighbors stepped in to push him away from me.

During the holidays, endless tasks were piled on my shoulders. My entire day was filled, leaving me only a few minutes to exchange a few words with my friend Sami Ben Hasqail. Sometimes I helped him make cars out of the baling wire saved for us by our friend Hamu the porter in return for our reading Egyptian magazines to him. I began my work with my father in the morning. I soaked the baskets, fans, and brooms he expected to sell that day in water from the Tigris, a task that took me more than two hours. Then I hurried to the Mad Dog's place and was busy for the rest of the day carrying out his commands. My work was rewarded with a variety of insults, beginning with simple name-calling: "Jackass! Donkey! Fool!" He was better at vile words than anyone else I have ever met. If anything escaped from me, even a look, he would become annoyed and would carry out his favorite task with slaps and punches.

One day I had been drinking warm water from the jug of Abu Gurwa the *chaichi* in the inn near the Mad Dog's shop. A *chaichi* was a tea-seller who in the summer gave free water from a porous clay jug that—if given time—cooled the water by evaporation. Frequent refilling on hot days, however, did not leave time for the water to cool. When I got back to the shop I saw a poor woman in an old tattered cloak and veil. With her was a little girl about the same age as Selam and I. The woman was pointing to the girl's dress, which was patched and torn in several places, showing her pale skin. The woman was beseeching the Mad Dog and the cloth merchants who were with him: "May God cover you sirs, she's an orphan with nothing to cover her and the holiday is coming. Make her happy, and may God make your children happy." She went on in this vein. Nobody looked at her. The Mad Dog was talking with another neighbor, as if she wasn't there. I realized that he and his neighbors had no intention of helping her. I moved out of his sight and stood in the woman's path. When she passed me I said, "Come with me. There's someone who can help you."

The veils that women wore in those times covered their features and whatever expressions they held. But I heard the woman shower me with blessings. I pointed furtively to my father's shop in the distance and said, "Try over there."

We were poor but my father was greatly respected. He was a religious man who refused to make money from his religion. He refused to take a salary from the Directorate of Endowments for serving as imam at the Sheikh Muhammad Mosque near our house, where Mullah Abdul-Hamid taught the neighborhood children. He also refused to become a mukhtar (district mayor). Mukhtars received a salary from the government, which collected money from the taxes levied on the sale of alcohol and prostitution. However, alcohol and prostitution were unlawful in Islam, and thus the government's money was unlawful. This abstinence won my father an unequaled reputation.

The woman repeated to my father what she had said to the Mad Dog. He interrupted her before she could finish and pointed to Hasqail's shop next door. "Go there." He called out to Hasqail. Hasqail, my friend Sami's father, cut three ells of cheap colored *sheet*. The woman took them, thanking him and blessing him. Then my father gave Hasqail three dirhams—a hundred and fifty fils—as I watched the transaction from a distance, glad that my father didn't know that I had instigated the whole thing.

I don't know why I thought of Selam after the woman left. I remembered her tight, tattered, worn-out dress full of patches. How could I buy her a dress for the holiday? How could I make her happy? I didn't have a hundred and fifty fils. My daily wages were only five fils. Where could I get this great sum? If her mother hadn't been sick, I would have asked her to come and approach my father as the other woman had. I was confident that my father would help her. He would give her what he had given the woman. But Selam's mother couldn't move. What, then, was to be done?

Most of the cloth that the merchants of Mosul dealt with in those days was imported from Britain. Then, that summer, a new commodity was imported which the Atami market had never seen before: the first batch of Japanese cloth arrived. It was no better than the English cloth, but it was cheaper. We sold Lion-brand English white calico (cotton cloth), with a picture on it of a lion opening its mouth, at 110 fils per ell (one ell = 28 inches), most often to be used as a shroud for the dead. It was called *khazna*. Now we were surprised by Japanese *khazna* of the Three Goldfish brand, lighter and narrower, for only 70 fils. The poor embraced it, and no one would buy British *khazna* anymore.

Then another kind of Japanese cloth arrived: a batch of printed artificial silk, in many brand names and marvelous, amazing patterns. It swept aside any similar English cloth that got in its way. The Japanese showed incomparable skill in imitation, creativity, and embellishment. On the label of every bolt of cloth they put a picture of a girl with European features, not Japanese: an extremely beautiful blonde girl, which was more than the English could manage. We children took up the hobby of collecting the pictures of beautiful girls. A few days before the holiday, the Mad Dog brought in a marvelous, amazing roll of

Japanese artificial silk taffeta. I can still remember its astonishing brilliant colors: violet shading to an exquisite blue, fire red dappled with light sky blue, and two borders—one of them black and the other gold. The beauty of the colors enchanted me and I wished I could buy Selam a dress made of it, but what could I do? Suddenly the notion of theft flashed in my mind, the urge to steal, for the first time in my life.

The Mad Dog usually ate lunch in the shop. He would order me to bring him kebab from Sayyid Bakr, the best *kebabji* in Mosul, whose restaurant was opposite the municipal building, at the entrance to the smiths' and potters' souk. But he stopped doing that, perhaps because he sensed people were muttering about his eating in front of me while I sat there hungry, watching him. Then he took to leaving me in the shop while he went to Sayyid Bakr's restaurant and ate his kebab there, with their excellent grape juice. And when he got back I would go to my father's shop to eat bread and watermelon or bread and grapes with him, as my father was poor compared to the Mad Dog, who made ten times what my father made.

In winter, which lasts three whole months in Mosul, my father didn't manage to sell anything worth mentioning. During those lean months every year he would have to borrow money from the wealthier merchants in the market, who respected him. In summer, however, when work blossomed with the harvest, he managed to pay back what he had borrowed in the winter.

I began praying to God that the Mad Dog would go to the restaurant that day so that I could steal some cloth for Selam. But he didn't go. Instead, he ordered me to go with one of the customers to bring money from the wheat wholesaler at Bab Sinjar. That was very far away and would take me an hour to get there and another to get back. Then he gave me ten fils for lunch.

Because I was so hungry, I bought a big loaf of bread and ate it all while I was following the peasant, who walked fast, forcing me to run after him. I got back in the afternoon and saw a large watermelon which had been left in his shop. He pointed at it and snarled, "Take it to my house." I put it on my shoulder and took it there, which was also far away. When I got back, evening was falling, and he was preparing to close the shop. And so he managed by this mean-spirited forced labor to kill the joy I would have had at meeting Selam that day.

The next day, a load of brooms arrived from Kerbala, packed in the form of a sort of bale that contained five hundred brooms, small and large. It was thrown down in the marketplace, and it was my job to carry them up to my father's storeroom: fourteen steps up from the street, and then to the left into a yard only a couple of meters square—which was shared by Hasqail's storeroom on the left and Safi's on the right—and then I had to take them five more steps up to our storeroom and arrange them neatly until they reached the ceiling, which was only a few centimeters more than a meter high. I took them up ten brooms at a time; the severe difficulty emerges from going up and down constantly—in addition to being pricked by the sharp palm leaves on my face, arms, and hands. The tips were pointed and as sharp as a needle. After taking the whole load of brooms up to the storeroom, I returned home with no fewer than a hundred little puncture wounds spread all over my body, and in each wound was a drop of dried blood.

I finished that day around noon, and I was surprised by the arrival of the Mad Dog. He sent me to Mary the seamstress with more than ten men's and women's robes. In spite of my hunger and fatigue, I was glad, because I had a chance, before going on the errand to Mary the seamstress, to sit in his shop and do what

I had intended, because he was going to the restaurant. I waited impatiently for that moment. As soon as he left, I took the most beautiful length of Japanese taffeta, the gorgeous one, and I cut off three ells of cloth and wrapped it up with care and put it in the pocket of my dishdasha. It didn't show at all. When the Mad Dog came back from the *kebabji's* he had a roll of bread in his hand containing onion and celery and a single shish kebab the size of a thumb. I was convulsed with hunger, and I ate it in the wink of an eye. Before I had finished it, he told me to take a piece of cloth to Mary the seamstress and then to go back to the wheat wholesaler in Bab Sinjar, because the dealer had asked me the previous day to postpone collecting until today.

I toddled off to Mary the seamstress's. I asked her to make the piece of taffeta into a dress for a girl about my age. I told her that I would pay for the sewing and asked her not to mention it to the Mad Dog. From the cubicle where she sat out of sight of the street, her sister Madeleine asked me, "Is it for your sister?"

"No."

I used to write letters from Madeleine's dictation to her fiancé Diya', who was studying at the university in Baghdad. Madeleine laughed. Winking, she asked me, "Who's it for, then?"

"A neighbor of mine."

"Come here."

I went up the three steps which separated her from the courtyard. She was sitting behind a sewing machine in her light muslin dress, which barely concealed the riches beneath. She gestured for me to sit near her. That made me so happy I almost passed out. My eyes wandered over the unknown territory of her splendid body, alluring and seductive. The dress revealed a great deal of her full breasts; above them a beautiful and elegant gold cross swung idly. In a trance, my eyes fixed on the marvel of her wondrous body, and I forgot the blazing heat and the endless running and fatigue. Madeleine finished a hem and of course caught me gaping at her. She seared me with a sharp look. I was embarrassed. I don't know if she noticed my red ears or not, but I felt them burning. But she relaxed her severe look and put her arms around me, closed her eyes again, and chuckled. "Oh, you little devil!"

I almost died of embarrassment. She said cheerfully, "I'll sew it for you for free, as a gift from me to you. Put the cloth here."

I put it next to her. Then I hurried off to the grain dealer's. The next day, I bought from Sasson a pair of beautiful blue sandals. They were special because they had a cord that separated the big toe from the others. They were the first sandals to arrive from outside the country. I bought them for ten fils. I paid him five fils and promised to pay the rest after the holiday. They were very cheap, but the cord came apart quickly. The sandal fell off if the cord was not carefully tied. I kept the sandals at my father's. My intention was to go and see Selam and enjoy her delight at the dress and the sandals. I was even dreaming of going with her to the cinema on the first day of the Great Feast. But the Mad Dog planted me in his shop until the evening and went with a broker to see a big piece of land he had bought in partnership with one of the larger merchants. He was hoping to sell it for ten times the price after it was divided.

My desire to see the joy in Selam's eyes when I gave her the new dress and the sandals was growing by the day, hour, and minute. I dreamed that the Mad Dog would set me free. The next day my nose started to bleed. I was forced to run to the mosque to put my head under the cold water faucet. My nose bled a lot in the summer. After I had been running around under the blazing sun for a while, my head would almost explode. No one knew that the right way to treat a nosebleed was by putting pressure on the nose. They always told us to put our heads under cold water for a few minutes. That worked most of the time, but only after losing a lot of blood.

In spite of that, I took the opportunity to flee from the Mad Dog. As soon as the bleeding stopped, I hurried to my father's shop and grabbed the bag containing the holiday dress and the sandals. I told my father I was going home. He had seen my dish-dasha soaked with water and knew that I had had a nosebleed. He shook his head in sympathy and said nothing.

I took a route that avoided the Mad Dog's shop. But as soon as I left my father's, I ran into Sami, who asked if I was in a hurry. When I said I was, he said, "I've been looking for you." Then he grinned. "I wanted to tell you the story of Samson the Mighty. I saw the movie yesterday. Was it ever great! Imagine, he was so amazingly strong he knocked down two giant pillars with his bare hands!"

I had seen the poster for the film. They used to put up lots of posters for movies a day or two before the Eid. I had put the film on my agenda for the holiday. It was interesting to hear Sami tell me the story of the film, but I couldn't wait around. As there were only a few days left before the holiday, the shopping crowd around Bab Al-Toub was at its greatest, and we were shouting at each other because of the noise of the crowd. I told him I was running away from the Mad Dog for a little while, and that we could meet the next day. He said gloomily, "You know I can't see you during the holiday." I knew that, but it had slipped my mind. I smiled and waved to him. But he came along with me, telling me about something from the movie, all the way to Bab Al-Toub.

When I finally shook him, I began to run with all my strength, driven by my longing. I stopped near the alley, hesitating; the whirlwind of joy that enveloped me was suffused with Selam. I was thinking only of her.

I didn't find her waiting for me as she had before at the mouth of the alley in the shade of the wall, leaning on it, the strain of waiting clouding her lovely black eyes. I wasn't worried; that was to be expected, as I had not been with her for four whole days. The ancient door was open as usual. I hurried in as I had done every other time. But what was this? I was amazed. Three little children, the smallest of them about six months old, and the others perhaps three and five, were sitting on a mat in the shade. A girl about seven, another about my age, and two girls older still, were making a tremendous noise playing around the well. Two of the older girls were sitting on the parapet of the well. I shouted, "Where's Selam?"

They were all startled by my entrance and my question. Silence suddenly reigned. They stared at me in astonishment.

"Where's Selam?"

I stared back at them and then I looked at the door of the room; maybe Selam was inside and would hear my voice and come out. I cried out weakly, searching for her mother: "Where's Selam's mother?"

A tall woman came out of the room. Around her waist was a sash like those worn by the peasant women around Mosul. A black turban made of *ibrisam,* a kind of silk, was wound loosely around her head, setting off the pallor of her face. She smiled tenderly and said, "Who is Selam, my child?"

Her oldest daughter—who was around sixteen, parted her hair in the middle, and had two black braids just like Selam— said, "We came yesterday. There was nobody here."

Another girl about my age said, "They went away three days ago, in the afternoon."

The life was crushed out of me. I didn't know what to say. My tears began to flow. I must have started to tremble; I must have looked pitiful. The eldest daughter said gently, "Don't cry."

Loud voices were raised, all at once. One of them said, "Poor thing, his robe is all bloody." Another asked, "Did somebody hurt you?" I felt one of them wiping the tears from my cheek with her fingers and repeating, "Don't cry. Be a man."

I got control of myself. But I was too upset for that to last. I took a deep breath. I saw the oil tin in its place, but it was dented. Perhaps the little children had been playing with it.

I put the paper bag on the parapet of the well. I climbed up on the oil tin, as everyone watched me with curiosity. I stretched out my hand, reaching into in the hole. I felt the rag and pulled it out, wrapped carefully just as Selam had left it. I put it in my pocket. Nobody did anything to stop me. I ran out. As soon as I was out the door the tears welled in my eyes again. Something inside me had perished and was lost. I couldn't walk. I stopped and leaned on the wall. I felt a tender hand caress my head, and a gentle voice said, "Is she a relative of yours?"

I turned to see the oldest girl. Before I could answer she was followed by the rest of them. They gathered around me in the alley. One of them handed me the paper bag. "This is yours. You forgot it."

"Poor boy."

Pushing the bag away, I said, "Take it. It's for you."

I slipped away then and started running, wiping my tears on the sleeve of my dishdasha. Then I slowed down. I didn't know where I was going. I wanted to be by myself, to try to answer the questions that were burning me up inside: Where had Selam and her mother gone? What had happened to them? Why did they leave the house? One of the girls had said, "They went away in the afternoon." That meant she had waited for me until the afternoon of the following day.

In those days no one could find a place to be alone. Our house was small. I couldn't just sit at home and think about anything. Where could I go? If I came home and was quiet, everyone would know that I was having some kind of crisis and would gather around me. So I had to hold back my tears and walk around aimlessly. The weight of the rag bundle in my pocket made me open it. I took out Selam's treasure. Her eyes had shone with joy and pride whenever she opened the bundle. The beautiful stones lay in my hand. So she must have left them for me. My eyes welled with tears again. There were also two pieces of paper, carefully folded. The first paper was the drawing of me standing with the rope in my hand, shaking the branch of the mulberry tree. She was standing near me, her back recognizable with the two braids thrown over it. On the second paper were my name and hers, written in large letters which almost filled the sheet, as if she were saying to me: "We are together in spirit."

I went on wandering at random, bewildered. I don't know how long I was drifting, lost in my memories of Selam. When I got back to the house and pushed the door open, my sister Shafaq was sweeping the courtyard. But as soon as her eyes fell on me she stopped, threw down the broom, straightened up in alarm, and rushed to embrace me. She asked, "What happened to you?"

"Nothing."

She kissed me, and then whispered, "No, something's wrong. What is it? Tell me, love."

I started to cry. She laughed, pinched my cheek, and said, "Why did you say 'nothing'?"

I mastered myself and repeated, "Nothing."

Sitting on the steps and pulling me onto her lap, she said, "All right, smile. Don't tell me. I'll believe you."

I smiled. She kissed me again. Then she went back to sweeping the yard, to get it clean before my father got home from evening prayer.

When I now think of Selam's sudden disappearance—more than half a century later—I relive those frantic moments, and pain constricts my heart. Could there be anyone poorer in all creation than that wretched pair, Selam and her mother? There was not a stick of furniture in their house, not even the most worthless, except for the ragged mat on which her mother lay. They had no gas cookstove or any utensils. None of the things for making tea that were found in any Iraqi household. They had one small aluminum dish on which Selam served me berries, and one small aluminum cup from which to drink water. Whenever she went into the room, I would follow her just to stick my head in, and I never saw anything, not even an old blanket. How did they live? They were the poorest family I ever saw in my life, perhaps the poorest family in existence. Before I saw Selam, I thought that Sabika, who lived in a ruined house, was the poorest creature in existence. But I had found someone who was poorer. Sabika had a box in which she kept a few cushions and blankets. She had a cookstove and cooking utensils. Selam and her mother had nothing. Our city was a city of the poor, and they used to say, "We have nothing but God's mercy." And I don't know what they meant by "God's mercy." Their souls? Life? Health? Then those two weak creatures didn't even have God's mercy. Her mother was so sick that she couldn't produce any sound, and Selam was thinner than any child I had ever seen.

After that I blamed myself greatly. If I had escaped the Mad Dog's vigilance I could have seen her and her mother. I could have found out what happened to them. I should have rebelled against the Mad Dog. He might have hit me cruelly when he saw me, but then at least I would have enjoyed my freedom. The trip to and from the grain warehouse at Bab Sinjar took more than two hours. If I hadn't gone, and had gone instead to my father and told him about Selam and her mother, he could have done something. If he had known about these two wretched people, he would have spoken with the mukhtar, or with some of the higher authorities, as he always did when he came across a poor person whom he was unable to help. He would have been able to help them, or to find someone who could have taken care of them. But because of my stupidity I accomplished nothing but a copious flow of tears. What pains me inside—to this day—is that I don't know what happened to them.

When, after that, I saw what happened to Madeleine, my pain and self-reproach grew deeper. But what happened to the most beautiful and brightest girl I ever saw in my life? I still don't know.

I kept the pebbles and the drawing for a long time, until I left Mosul. I don't know what happened to the pebbles. But I lost the drawings in 1963, when I was arrested in a city in the south. I was arrested in the street and was only released a year and a day later, and I don't know what happened to my possessions, my books, and the plans for the novels and stories that I was writing at the time.

For a long time, without wanting to, every time I closed my eyes at night before I went to sleep, I heard Selam's words repeated in my deepest being: *Close your eyes and try to see me. Then you'll be able to draw me like I did you.*

Yes, I can see her. I see her as she was, but my eyes well with tears again every time I try to draw her. My vision clouds and I can't go on.

PART FIVE

The Ravishing Madeleine

Madeleine was a rare beauty—a gracefully voluptuous figure, reddish coffee-brown hair, fair skin, and dimples on both cheeks. Her melodious laugh, like the clinking of crystal, had always raised my spirits to the sky. Soaring, I would close my eyes and roam God's seven heavens, until my soul dissolved in the sweetness of the tune. The ravishing Madeleine sometimes hugged me and showered me with kisses. We were left alone together numerous times, and she granted me glimpses of charms that no one else besides her fiancé Diya' ever got to see. Her kisses were sweet, but different from those of Selam—who I felt was a part of me—and from those of Sumaya, who, before she left, was to propel me into adolescence.

I believe none of my peers ever had the chance to meet a beauty like Madeleine. She was a treasure that enriched my spirit and a tragedy that blistered my heart, torturing me still like the memories of Selam and Sumaya. Pure and vibrant memory wavers between two eternal foes: immeasurable bliss and unbearable pain. Maybe this is simply the nature of life.

The friendship began one day in summertime when I delivered fabric to her house. Mary and Madeleine were having a heated conversation. I hesitated in the doorway. I wouldn't have walked in if the door had been closed. But their front door was always open. I was only to see it closed once.

Mary was there sitting in the heart of the courtyard, a big golden cross shining on her chest. All the passersby descending the twenty steps or more that made up the wide street opening into the public square could glance in and see her sewing clothes. The house was built from *al-farsh,* a bluish-white Mosul alabaster. The courtyard was about two by four meters, and Mary was hunched over an old Pfaff hand sewing machine in front of the family room. Two steps up and to the right, Madeleine sat in a similar space, in front of her bedroom. Perhaps she chose that spot seeking some privacy, especially during summer where she would be almost naked in a thin, revealing muslin robe. Their mother was perched on a rattan chair by the entrance to a lower-level room, also accessible via two steps, operating a Singer pedal foot sewing machine.

I was the delivery boy for a draper, bringing Mary the day's consignment of goods to be sewn. She handled the business dealings for her mother and sister Madeleine. She would negotiate a deal and record it in her poor handwriting, a series of scribbles nobody but her and God could understand. Mary was one of dozens of seamstresses who sewed robes for the Arab and Kurdish villagers. (The Assyrians, Jews, Aramaeans, Turkmen, Yazidis, and Shabak used the services of tailors in their own villages.) Those farmers flooded into Mosul every summer after harvest. They would come in throngs of hundreds upon hundreds to buy fabric for their entire family and have it sewn into robes, and then head back.

Many drapers cheated the poor peasants in several ways. They used to charge them 120 fils to sew a *jallabiyah* or dishdasha while they would pay the seamstress only 70 or 80 fils. A few of them were honest and paid as charged. But the Mad Dog belonged to the first category. Mary and Madeleine were terrified of him. He was as hard as a rock. He used to skim off part of their and their mother's hard work. The only one he didn't cheat was Umm Ghanem, because he was afraid of her brother, who owned the store he was renting. This exploitation pained me as much as it did the seamstresses. I expected he would reward them for the long hours of work, for meeting deadlines, and for mastering their job, but he insisted on skimming 50 fils if the total bill was around one dinar (a dinar containing a thousand fils) and 100 fils if the total was around 2 dinars. This extortion couldn't have been for the purpose of making him rich, because he was already very wealthy. So I suggested to Mary that she fudge the number of pieces she charged him for sewing.

"That would be dishonest. How can I tell him it's thirty pieces when it's actually twenty-nine?"

"It's your right. It's not dishonest. He's already taking money from you. Ask any clergyman, Muslim or Christian."

She must have consulted a pastor after she pondered my words. The next day when I brought her a new batch of fabric, she asked, "What if he discovers I'm fudging the number of pieces I sew?"

"Don't worry; he won't be able to tell," I answered. "He doesn't write down the number of the pieces he sends out, unless he sells on credit. And still, he rarely checks his records. I'll vouch for you if he objects, and if he won't believe me, I'll have my father intervene."

I was thrilled when she went ahead with my suggestion. She was honest to a great extent—she would only increase the number of the pieces to offset as closely as possible the amount of money he was cutting. For instance, she would bill him for sixteen pieces on Thursday, twenty-seven pieces on Friday, and twenty on Saturday, while the reality was less by only one or two pieces.

The sewing and tailoring were very basic. The many times I watched Mary design, cut, and stitch gave me a very clear idea about this process, which I can describe with ease and accuracy, even if I could never have actually done it. The men's *thoub*, a robe-like garment, is plain, except for two long pockets on the right and left sides. The women's *jallabiyah* is similar, except for the long, wide sleeves that the lady could tie in the back in order to perform tasks such as milking, harvesting, cultivating, and so forth. Mary would record in a notebook the type of each piece and the tailoring fee. She was very meticulous, like any other skilled seamstress, and always attentive to her customers' demands.

That morning, Mary seemed nervous, turning from time to time to Madeleine to say something, and then resuming her sewing.

Suddenly, Mary blew up. "What am I supposed to do?" she yelled. "I can't help it if the girl can't come. She might have gotten sick, God forbid!" She crossed herself. "City Hall is just around the corner and there are plenty of clerks who could write a letter for you. Go right now."

"No . . ." I cried, raising my eyes toward Madeleine, who was about a meter away, two steps up. "I can write the letter for you."

The two of them fell silent, while their mother shot me a skeptical look from her spot in front of the lower room. Since I was in the middle, near Mary, I had to raise my head and turn to the right if I wanted to address Madeleine, and had to turn to the left and stare down if the mother was the one doing the talking.

The architect had to resort to this split-level design because the house and the street were located on a slope with at least a 30-degree angle. He had to use that gradient skillfully. Visitors would see an atrium two meters wide that led to Mary's room, and would have to climb two steps up to Madeleine's room or go down two steps to the mother's room.

"What grade are you in?" Madeleine asked. I turned and raised my eyes toward her. "Fourth grade," I answered. I lied of course, adding a year or two—I don't recall exactly.

Madeleine laughed softly, sarcastically. I felt ashamed, but the magic of her voice spun me, it bewitched me: I did not feel offended at all. Instead, I felt a keen pleasure and didn't care to return the insult. She eyed me skeptically. She hesitated and looked at Mary and her mother. "Enough!" Mary snapped.

"Come now, my daughter," her mother said encouragingly. "You're beating yourself to death."

Madeleine giggled again, but this time her laughter was companionable and drew me into the heart of her happiness.

"Come up here," she said.

Madeleine was around seventeen years old. Her fair skin had a warm red glow. She had exquisite eyebrows that could have been drawn by a great artist. I stole a glance at her. She was not a rare beauty like Selam, but she had a tremendous sweetness that almost made me want to nibble at her. I was nine years old and didn't know why I always wanted to look at her. I couldn't take my eyes off her, or, for that matter, any other pretty woman. The beauty of women had transfixed me since my earliest youth.

I felt immensely privileged as I went up to her. I couldn't believe my eyes. I was close to her. Was this really happening?

"Sit down," she said.

She brought me a cushion to sit on, with the German Pfaff machine in front of us. Mary was eying us from time to time. Madeleine didn't like that. She got up and pulled me by the hand.

"Come on," she said. I followed her into her bedroom. A cool dampness met my feet. The floor was made of marble, and they must have kept it sprinkled with water. My feet were bare and soiled with a layer of dry mud. I slipped back to the faucet in the courtyard and rinsed them with cold water and then went up to the room. I waited a few moments until my feet dried, Madeleine watching me with a smile.

She closed the door. The heat was suffocating. Our bodies and clothes became moist with sweat. After a moment's hesitation she hastened to open the door a little. Hot air flowed in and the situation became more tolerable. Alabaster normally keeps a house cool in summer, but that day it was like a furnace, except for the floor.

"Sit." She pointed to the cushion, while she sat on the floor.

"No, I'll sit on the floor, too. It's cooler," I said.

There were two tall windows that overlooked the sloping street. She opened them, and we faced the street directly. Anyone could see us, which she didn't like. She rolled down the curtains, but pulled a section aside to allow some air to get through. The air was better, but the heat was still brutal.

I could see through her transparent muslin dress, the swell of her splendid breasts with the dark nipples, and the elegant cross hanging from a thin gold chain swinging playfully between them. Thinking back to that era, I can attest that the middle-class women of my society didn't know the brassiere, although I used to see it displayed in several exciting colors in the stores of Serjakhana.

"How old are you?" she asked when she saw me staring avidly at her body.

"Ten."

I added a year, as I had done before. She chuckled and pinched me playfully on my cheek. "You little imp! You're so young."

I didn't know what she meant, but she spread her legs wide, and rolled up her muslin dress, exposing her beautiful thighs. I had never before seen any exposed part of a woman, except in the magazines that Hamu asked me to read for him. That sudden human nudity overwhelmed me. Her body was like a bottle of pure milk, harmonious in the extreme. Her breasts jutted like two birds preparing to fly. Her waist was narrow, dimpled with a deep captivating navel, her rounded haunches diverging into beautiful thighs. I was acutely, oppressively, aware of her beauty, making me want to kiss every single inch of that body—moist with beads of pure, enticing sweat—exposed before me, dissolving me inside, and forcing me to exercise the patience of Job to refrain from lapping it up.

She held out both hands and drew me in between her legs. Then she took two sheets of paper from a notebook thrown on the bed and laid them on top of it. She handed them to me along with a pencil.

"Write," she urged me.

The room had become a hellhole; I almost fainted from the heat. My head started to spin. Perhaps Madeleine sensed my suffering. She got up immediately, opened the door, and jumped down the three steps like a lioness. She took the black Japanese KDK fan that her mother was using and came back chuckling, victorious. The atmosphere soon became more bearable. She also brought chilled water in a glass pitcher and rewarded me with a full cup that I drank in a flash. What I drank turned immediately into sweat that oozed from me and soaked my dishdasha. She offered me another cup that I gulped down. She also slugged down two full cups of water. Only then did my head clear.

I was ready to write, endlessly and effortlessly. She sat again on the floor, spreading her legs, exposing her lovely, shapely thighs, so that I saw red silk cloth between them. This was something new, something remarkable and different. What a delight it was to see the legs and thighs of a girl and what was between them. I had seen something similar in the Egyptian magazines such as *The Latest Hour* and *The Photographer* that Hamu had borrowed from Kheiri, the prominent merchant. I would read for him the news of Samia Jamal and other artists, and the captions under the pictures. The most I ever saw were the photos of females sunbathing on the Mediterranean coast of Alexandria. But I had never seen an alluring body like Madeleine's exposed in reality. I had never been close to any mature girl who was anything but fully clothed. My sisters and relatives used to cover their bodies from head to toe. When going out, they would wear a black cloak that veiled every single inch, and they slept in a room separate from my and my brother's. Sitting there with Madeleine, I smelled the intoxicating female scent, as strong as a scent could be: delicious, pungent, and overwhelming.

My presence between Madeleine's legs, so close to her, shook me, scattered my wits, and ripened my body prematurely. It was an eternal moment that showed me how a female could affect the male, be he a child or an adult, and with what power! But I didn't realize it at the time.

"Write! Where did you go?" she exclaimed.

Then she held my shoulders with her two hands and shook me gently. "Don't think badly of me and drag my name in the mud," she said, almost imploring. "It's for my fiancé, Diya'."

A fit of shyness overcame me. The agitation had no doubt turned my ears as red as beets. Perhaps she noticed that. She let go of me. "You're bashful. You're a good boy who won't peddle lies. I trust you."

My tongue was palsied. "I won't say a single word," I said moments later, flustered.

She rested the book on the floor in the small space between me and her thighs. It almost touched the small piece of red cloth in the center, but that position was not suitable for writing, so she lifted it up and placed it on my folded knees. "Well done," she said, grinning. Then came the second order, "Write: 'My sweetheart.'"

I tried to write these two words in a style of Arabic calligraphy called *naskh ta'liq,* but she snatched the notebook and the paper sheets from my hand. "You're playing; you're scribbling!" she yelled. "I believed you; I thought you knew how to write!"

She stood up, upset and on the brink of tears. She went down to Mary and told her in a wavering voice, "Look what he did. He's scribbling. He doesn't know how to write. You said he knows!"

I was supremely embarrassed. How could I defend myself? The two sisters were barely literate. I decided to leave. I got up and stood in the doorway, ready to go down the two steps. Mary stared at my script. She was in her late twenties, with fair skin and an oblong face with a receding chin that distorted her features and marred the beauty of her face. She cried, "Oh, God! What fine handwriting!" She scolded Madeleine. "You're mad! This is the best writing I've ever seen. It's like Mohammed Fawzi's, the famous calligrapher."

Mary had saved me, but my feelings had been hurt. I stepped down to leave, but Madeleine rushed to me. She hugged me, laughing cheerfully and kissing me on the cheek. "Don't be upset, sweetheart."

Mary laughed. "How many sweethearts do you have, you silly thing?"

I forgot Madeleine's insults instantly, since hugging her was the sum of my desires. Her closeness melted me. Her lips lighted on my cheek; the intense female scent was like the smell of wild herbs.

When we sat again in the same place, she held my cheeks in her hands and said, "You're not upset with me, are you?" Then, she sang in a sweet voice:

"Don't kiss me on the eyes,
Kissing on the eyes will drive us apart . . ."

I felt bashful. She smiled. I kept staring at her, melting in the soul-stirring voice. "Write. I told you to write," she cried suddenly. "Why are you just sitting there?"

"What shall I write?"

"What you heard."

"The song?"

"Yes, the song: *Don't kiss me on the eyes, kissing on the eyes will drive us apart.* He used to kiss me here and here," she whispered, pointing to her eyes. "He would kiss me and sing along."

I wrote down the line of the song the best I could.

"Light, my darling."

"Light? Is that his name?" I asked.

"Have you ever known anyone named Light? It's Diya', which means light. Can't you see the world lit up?"

I was flustered again, but I didn't say a word. She caressed my face with her warm, sweet palm and whispered to herself, "Am I crazy? I'm giving away the secrets of the person dearest to me!"

That was apparently a dilemma that required a quick resolution. My heart quivered, fearing that she would decide to stop dictating the letter, and kick me out of her infernal paradise. She fixed my eyes with hers. "Do you love me?" she asked.

"Yes."

"Like a sister?"

"Sure."

She hugged me, and my whole body flamed from the heat and excitement.

"I love you too, like a little brother."

"Write."

We kept writing until the page was filled.

"That's enough. Read."

I read for her what I had written. I had changed the structure of some sentences. She cried out as she hugged me once more, "You're better than Sournam, my fifth-grader friend!" She curled her lips in disdain. "She plays hoity-toity, as if no one else knows how to write."

She rushed down to Mary, happy as could be. "Did you see what he wrote?" she cried. "He's smart—his words are good enough to be on the radio."

I stepped out of the room, soaked in sweat. I let out a sigh of relief.

"I told you," Mary said to her sister, eyeing me with admiration.

"You told me to go to a clerk," Madeleine added. "Do you think I could have asked him to write for me, *'Your love has taken over my mind! I'm in love, I'm in love!'*? He would have laughed at me and spread my secret all over the neighborhood!"

Writing for Madeleine forged my relationship with her. She would hug me every time I brought the fabric from the Mad Dog, and kiss me on the cheeks the same way Selam did. She would turn a blind eye to my wild, furtive glances that pierced the thin muslin dress and got lost in the beauty of her exquisite body, especially her wonderful breasts, which made me fight a fierce urge to touch them. We used to chat about various things. One day I brought her some of the pictures of spectacular blondes that the textile factories used to stick on each fabric roll. She rejoiced, and the following day she hung them in her room, one next to the other.

I met Selam around the same time that Madeleine and I became close. Madeleine offered to sew a cloak for her and refused to charge me a penny. I felt great pride because there was one person who recognized my talents and reciprocated my favors. When she learned that the school year was nearing and that I wouldn't go to the souk as often, she begged me to visit with them once a week at least, as she might need another letter. That was a pleasure and a privilege.

Madeleine was always stationed in front of her bedroom, with the Pfaff machine between her legs, her dress pulled up to her thighs. She often caught me looking with innocent pleasure at her naked thighs and what was between them, at her nipples, and at the lucky cross that swung playfully between them with eternal lust. But she would only pull me gently by my ear, while smiling and whispering low so that neither Mary nor her mother would hear her, "You little imp . . . You're so young."

That created between us a thrilling, secret collusion, anointed with promises and pleasure. I doubt that Mary ever discovered the love I had for Madeleine. I tried to linger in that house to absorb her beauty. I would make up any excuse to stay longer. I often distracted Mary by bringing up topics beyond her knowledge. There were three paintings hanging in the courtyard, one above the door of each room, which were familiar to me because they were displayed in most coffee shops and stores. The first one was of Mar Kourkis, the courageous saint of Mosul, conqueror of the huge dragon. The second one was of Jesus Christ with his usual benevolent features. The third one was of a naked child in the arms of the Virgin Mary. I often used these paintings to strike up conversations with Mary, with the aim of tarrying near Madeleine, who would look at me and smile cleverly, as if she were enjoying the presence of an admirer, even if he was a child.

I finished writing the letter and in return got a handsome reward —another kiss on my cheek and ten fils. I still remember that kiss, but I turned down the money. When she insisted that I take it, I answered her, "I won't write for you again if you keep insisting."

A week later, no sooner had I walked into the courtyard and she laid eyes on me, than she got up and cried, "Come on, sweetheart, hurry up."

"What a lunatic," Mary and her mother said, laughing.

I set the fabric down next to Mary. There were about twenty pieces, with no special requests from the customers. Mary could tell what to sew from the type of fabric. If it was crepe satin, taffeta, chintz, or synthetic silk, then it would be a *jallabiyah* for women or girls. If it was classic calico cotton, poplin, or a cheaper imitation of cashmere, then it would be a dishdasha for men or boys.

Madeleine told me gleefully—cheeks glowing—that Diya' thought she had hired the services of a calligrapher to write the letter for her. He found the handwriting stunning, but the content mattered more to him. He also believed she shouldn't go to the trouble of going to a calligrapher. She laughed heartily. "Do you know what else he said?"

"No."

She smiled. "He said I shouldn't let the calligrapher write for me. Apparently, he thinks I paid him a fortune." She laughed. "Write him that it's true that I paid you a fortune and tell him: 'Madeleine kissed me on the cheek.'"

Before she could go on, her mother, overhearing our conversation, shouted, "You silly girl, he'll think a young man helped you with the letter and he'll be furious. Will you ever come to your senses?"

She laughed joyfully, ignoring her mother. She held my hand and together we went to her room. We sat on the floor just like the first time.

"Write," she urged.

"No, I won't write that," I replied.

She pulled my ear gently and gnashed her teeth. "How smart of you!"

Throughout the course of our friendship, I never got to meet Diya'. However, he was vividly with us. I came to know everything about him: his favorite food; the style of clothes he liked; his major at the university; how he spent his time; the names of his aunt and her husband, the seller of the most famous *kibbeh* in Baghdad; and the names of their three boys and two girls. Madeleine's eyes glittered at the mention of his name. I used to rejoice for her whenever she received a letter from him, and would worry when the letter was a week late—then I would stay for only a few minutes and leave disheartened. She used to get depressed over such delays and her smile would fade. One time I noticed her eyes swollen red with tears, and learned that Diya' hadn't written her for over a month. I left immediately, because I knew if I greeted her she would cry and I would be heavy-hearted.

The weather became more moderate and deprived me of the enjoyment of looking at her splendid body. She wore a turquoise blouse over her white pajamas. I used to visit with them for half an hour during winter, and always got royal treatment. They all pampered me, offering me tea and cookies. Even Mary volunteered to sew shirts for me that were better than the ones in the market. One day I bought from Hasqail two yards of nice, striped fabric, which my father paid for. Mary turned them into a gorgeous summer shirt with two pockets. My friend Ghanem loved that shirt, although he was used to wearing whatever his mother tailored for him.

Around spring break, I learned that Madeleine had gone with Diya' to Kermlis. He had come from Baghdad to visit with his parents. That was his last year at the university. He would be graduating at the end of the school year. I left her house right away, feeling an intense desolation. The house was lifeless without her laughter, her brisk gestures, and her alluring perfume.

I missed meeting him when they came back from their trip, since he left early for Baghdad. But I saw Madeleine, and she was a glowing volcano of love. From then on, if I recall correctly, I wrote only two more letters for her. Her love for him had reached the point of obsession. Diya' had told her that he had come close to fulfilling his aspirations and that he was expecting to win a scholarship because he believed he was the best in his class. He also said that everyone was predicting a bright future for him as a university mathematics professor.

One day when I showed up with a consignment of fabric, Madeleine stopped sewing the minute she saw me. "Where have you been?" she cried. "I've been waiting for you. Come, don't you want to hear the latest news?" She took my hand and pulled me into her room, with Mary laughing at us while she sewed. I was tremendously embarrassed. I turned to her mother and she too was smiling discreetly. We didn't sit on the floor this time.

We sat on her bed, which had a pink cover and a beautiful pillow embroidered with flowers of colorful silk.

Madeleine was radiant. "You'll never guess what happened! Diya' has been nominated for a scholarship. They're going to send him to get a "Ph.D. in mathematics"—in London!"

This was tremendous news. Everything happened as expected. Diya' graduated, was nominated for a scholarship in Britain, and approval was granted after a very short period. Madeleine traveled with him once again to Kermlis, and then he dropped her off in Mosul and returned to Baghdad. He told her they would marry and travel together to London.

Madeleine's family started to prepare for the wedding ceremony in church. They had saved enough money to throw a glamorous reception and help the bride and groom start a new life abroad. That was like a dowry from the Christian bride to her husband. They started to discuss details with Diya''s parents such as the place of the party, the number of guests, the type of garments, and so forth.

Then they heard that he had traveled to Britain alone. Madeleine nearly went mad because she had been expecting to travel with him, as he had been promising her. However, Mary, her mother, and their friends assured her that it was better this way since he would undoubtedly be making the necessary arrangements to prepare for her arrival.

Madeleine calmed down after hearing her mother's and sister's justifications. Afterward, when I went to visit with her, she grabbed my hand and took me to her room. I had expected she would write him a letter, but instead she started to narrate something like a film about the future—wonderful rosy dreams and overwhelming female sentimentality, everything revolving around love. She pointed to her sister and mother. "I can't talk to them. They know nothing. You understand better. You read a lot. You know what I mean? I'm waiting for an air ticket. He went to London ahead of me. I'll join him there. I'll go to school while he pursues his goals. We'll buy a car; we'll go on an excursion to the countryside every Sunday. We'll see the world; we'll travel. He'll get his Ph.D.; he'll work abroad. We'll only come back to see our families. I won't sew anymore; I'll leave the sewing to seamstresses," she said. Then she fixed her eyes on mine and said, "I've become a Singer machine." She sighed, rotating her hand the way she would spin the sewing machine. "Even in my dreams, I see my hand revolving with the wheel."

From then on she began living in London in her mind. Her dreams had no end. "We'll be rich. We'll visit the US and France. We'll visit the big parks, the palaces of King George VI, the enormous bridges, the historic buildings. I'll throw away the *abaya* and wear fashionable clothes. He says I'm prettier than any English girl. The British girls will be jealous of me." She laughed heartily.

Less than a month after Diya''s departure for London, the disastrous letter arrived. It was the first letter the postman had ever delivered from Great Britain. I walked into her house the day after the letter arrived. Mary showed it to me, tears rolling down her cheeks. It included just a few short phrases, like a telegram: *"I am sorry, I cannot marry now. I cannot promise anything. Marriage would interfere with my future. I cannot say more."*

The sun didn't rise that day. The universe lay in darkness. The air was still. The whole world subsided into hell—nothing but grief and despair.

Mary would cry, blow her nose, quiet down, and then resume crying. As for Madeleine, she had torn her clothes, pulled her hair out, and fainted several times. When she came to, she refused to believe what had happened—she banged on the wall and pounded her thighs until her skin blistered, then dozed off in the late hours of the night. When she woke up after about an hour, she entered her room and closed the door. Mary and her mother feared she would kill herself with a knife or scissors, which were plentiful in that house. So Mary hid all the knives and scissors.

Madeleine didn't try to kill herself, which was a good sign. But she would come out of her room only to go to the bathroom, and then lock herself in her room. She didn't eat or drink for around a day and a half.

"She'll starve to death," her mother said.

I said, "I read once about some people lost at the North Pole without anything to eat for more than a week, but the rescue team found them alive."

I left. I convinced myself that she would forget Diya''s betrayal of her love and she would emerge stronger. She would go back to being gay, sprightly, radiant, and charming. She would revert to her previous state and fill the world with noise, joy, and love. I tried to resist a pressing desire to visit her daily. Her image, along with that of Selam and her mother, took over my mind. My heart contracted. I wished Madeleine was young, like Selam. I would have bought her marbles, or dessert, but she was too old for that.

After about four weeks, maybe less, she and Selam were constantly at the forefront of my mind; at night I actually dreamed they were embracing me. Then one afternoon, I was seized by an urge beyond my control to go see her. What if she needed me and I was away? I hurried to her house. The door was closed, which wasn't usual. My heart quailed. Her mother answered the door. When our eyes met, I saw immediately that something was wrong. Her face was contorted from holding back her tears. She did not utter a word as she led me in. Mary wasn't there. The mother stood on the landing and motioned, in complete silence, toward the door of Madeleine's room. I pushed the door open. Madeleine, pale, was lying on her pink bed, half of her weight gone in such a short time. She smiled when she saw me, and her eyes shone with a strange glitter. She sat up. It was late in spring, and by her side was a plate with one round piece of *hala-wat al-Khodr*, a type of sweet. It was intact; she hadn't touched it. I approached, taking off my shoes off before stepping on the Persian carpet. She opened her arms and pulled me close. She clutched me to her, having pulled the covers up to her waist. Then she put her lips on my cheek and started crying, soaking my face with her tears. "Enough, he doesn't deserve you," I said. "Why don't you forget him? He forgot you."

She stopped crying and pointed to the *halawa*. "Eat," she said. I refused. She insisted. "I eat if you eat," I replied. I handed her the plate, which was at my side. She cut off a small piece and placed it in her mouth. I did the same. The *halawa* was delicious, but she didn't eat any more. Neither did I.

"Why didn't you check on me before?" she asked, accusingly.

"I thought you got over him and you were back to normal."

"Do you love me?"

"From the bottom of my heart."

She laughed. "Then why did you stop visiting me?" she whispered.

I didn't answer. My heart was twisted in pain. I wished I could say what I wanted to say. I struggled, I smiled. She caressed my cheek.

"You're so young," she said.

I didn't know why she said that. For the longest time, I couldn't imagine. Her words were a mystery I couldn't solve, one of many riddles on a long list.

I felt the warmth of her meager body—her face resting on my chest, her thick hair brushing my chin, and her chest rising up and down as though it was part of me. She was breathing deeply like a small child. How could a young beauty, so open to love and life, come to a little boy like me to share her dreams, her future plans, and her downfall, without my feeling any pain? What I knew about her was not known to anyone else but Diya'. I felt her tears wet my chest. I raised her face and kissed her on the forehead. "Enough. Tears won't change anything. Don't wear yourself out brooding over him."

"I want to die; I have no hope in life."

I could tell she meant what she said. She would disappear the same way Selam had. It was only a matter of time. I wept silently and when she noticed that, she said, "I'm tired. I want to sleep."

I rose from the bed and pulled the cover up to her neck. Her extreme pallor and emaciated features were very similar to those of Selam's mother. I held my hand out to wipe her tears, but she turned her head away toward the wall. I knew she wanted me to leave. I left, closing the door quietly. Tears rolled down my cheeks. I made sure not to make any sound. I noticed that Mary had returned to her sewing machine. I didn't look at her. She stopped sewing and sat crying silently.

I went down the stairs. I sat by Mary; she wiped her eyes. She looked at me, the redness of her eyes dissipating their beauty. She then resumed her work. "Why is she doing this to herself?" I whispered. "There are thousands of men who would desire her. She's so beautiful. Why?"

"You're little and you don't know anything."

"I do, too. What's the matter?"

"Would you eat from a yogurt once the skin on top is broken?" she asked without looking at me.

Tears flowed again. I didn't understand the meaning of her words back then. But now after so many years of pondering, I understand what she meant.

I went back two days later, in the afternoon, and saw the door closed. When I knocked on it, no one answered. Then I planned to visit her the next day, but I had read in the latest issue of *Reader's Digest* that you should bring the patient a bouquet of flowers. Mosul had no florists back then. When I asked a friend of mine what else I could take with me, he suggested oranges. I was sure she would refuse to eat; also I didn't have the money for a kilogram of oranges. I stared at him and said nothing.

"Yes, oranges," he repeated. "At least one kilo. Why?"

"Nothing. Just a question."

I put off my visit for some time after that. I decided to collect enough money to buy a bottle of orange juice rather than a kilo of oranges. But it was impossible for me to save enough money. I used to forget and spend my allowance, which at the time was 10 fils. But I never for one moment stopped thinking about both Madeleine and Selam. I used to pass daily through the narrow street leading to Selam's place, and as soon as I remembered her, Madeleine also appeared to me.

The illness that linked Selam's mother and Madeleine had a great impact on me. They would come to my mind whenever I was alone. Perhaps that was the secret reason that finally pushed me toward her house one afternoon. I knocked on the door and a young nurse answered the door. My heart started to race. "Are you a family member?" he asked.

He tried to shut the door when I said no. I was hysterical and frantically pushed the door, crying, "Let me in! I have to see her." But I stopped. The courtyard was filled with people: a priest, around sixty years old; Mary and her mother, both crying and standing in front of the main room; and a few other strange, grieving women, some of them wiping their eyes. They were standing silent and subdued, as if waiting for something to happen.

"What happened to Madeleine?" I screamed, frantic. I darted to her room. The nurse seized me. "Stop! Don't go up there," he shouted. "You'll catch the infection. We're taking her to quarantine now."

I didn't understand what he meant by quarantine. I didn't want to understand. I opened the door of her room and rushed in. She was lying on the bed, eyes closed, her palms on her chest above the cover. Her figure was skeletal, almost without flesh, just like Selam's mother. There were the same remnants of facial features tinged a faded turmeric color. I grabbed her hand and felt only bones, but she was warm. She opened her eyes; they lit up. She recognized me! The specter of an endearing smile loomed on her face. Without thinking, I raised her hand to my lips and started kissing it, losing control, crying and whispering, "Madeleine, don't die; please, don't die."

Her smile became more radiant and I imagined that she blushed. Her eyes filled with tears. She turned her face toward the wall and I saw nothing but her reddish chestnut hair. Then she pulled her hand away with a surprising strength for such a weakened, wasted body. But she failed to return it to her chest, and instead, it dropped at the side of the bed.

I turned around. The priest, the nurse, and the strange women filled the doorway, looking at us. I sat on the carpet near the bed and burst out sobbing.

The nurse approached the bed. He was wearing white medical gloves. He extended his hand toward her face. I didn't see what he did. Then he turned toward the priest and the rest of the people. "She's gone," he said. "No need to take her to quarantine."

Then he reached out his hand and pulled me up. I got up. "Come with me. I'll sterilize your hands and give you pills against the infection," he said.

I cried out, "I don't need to!" But he wouldn't let go of me. At the same time, the wailing of women rose up to the skies.

Mary and Jameel

In the Bab Likish district, just before the street branches into two streets, stood one of the best furniture shops in Mosul. I hadn't seen it before, because it was located at the mouth of a small alley. When I passed it that morning I heard Hazim, whom I had known since eighth grade, calling me. When I approached him, he pointed to the shop and said "This is ours."

Above the shop was a sign, faded and nearly illegible. I could just make out the words, *Abu Mer'ee Carpentry.* I said, "Nobody can read that sign. Your father should get it repainted with some fancy calligraphy. That will pull in customers."

Hazim said, "My father's too busy to go to the calligrapher."

"I can do it, right here in the shop. All he has to do is get paint and brushes."

Three days later I was surprised to see Hazim waiting for me. He called to me over in front of the shop.

Somebody had taken down the sign. It was about one meter long and a half meter wide. A couple of employees were scraping the old paint from the sign and the frame. That was when I met

Hazim's father for the first time. From his smile I realized he had been expecting my arrival.

I asked Hazim to help me paint the sign. We painted the frame black and the background white. When we finished, we put the sign in the sun to dry. We would continue the next day, which was Thursday.

From long observation of Mohammed Fawzi, a local calligrapher, I had learned to first draw in pencil and then use oil paint.

Most of the signs in Mosul are written with one of two kinds of calligraphy, *Ruq'ah* or *Ta'liq*, also called Farsi. I preferred Farsi.

When I began I saw Hazim's father looking at me doubtfully. He asked me "Can you really do good calligraphy?"

"Yes."

He still looked skeptical. "Are you sure?"

Hazim intervened immediately, "He's at the top of the class in everything. He knows better than us."

His father interrupted him, "Shut up you jackass. You can't even write your own name."

Embarrassed and angry, I turned to leave, but Hazim's father caught me by the shoulder. "I'm like your father. Don't get mad. Write it however you want."

This was a big test for me. Working on the sign was like an exam. I had earned a modest reputation as a calligrapher and a top student, and I didn't want it ruined.

But when I started to write, I couldn't control the brush they had given me. It wobbled right and left and distorted the calligraphy. It was different from Mohamed Fawzi's brush, which was like a pencil and drew in a straight line.

I was afraid I would fail and my fear of losing my reputation would become real. The problem was a technical issue, and not my fault, but Hazim and his father didn't know that. I said to

Hazim, "This brush is no good. I'll go buy another one, a better one."

I went to the market. My first thought was to go ask Mohammed Fawzi where he got his brushes. But I canceled this idea. First, he was deaf. Second, I didn't want him to think that I was trying to compete with him.

Then, a few meters away, I saw a body shop man put a strip of adhesive tape on a windshield in order to shield it from the paint.

I got an idea. What if I wrote the words on paper, cut out the paper where the writing was, and then filled in the space with paint?

I went home and got to work. The next day I glued the paper to the board, let it dry in the sun, and then, after a while, I filled in the spaces with red oil paint. After I removed the paper only the calligraphy remained—clear, straight, and beautiful.

Abu Hazim was delighted when he saw it. He began to spell out the words. It seemed that he had trouble reading. He turned to me and asked, "What did you write?"

"Carpentry of the Future. Owner Muhammad Abu Mer'ee."

Laughing exuberantly, he put his hand in his pocket and offered me a hundred fils, but I refused to take them. He said to me, "Come here when you get out of school. I'll give you fifty fils a day, no matter how little you work, even if it's only half an hour."

Fifty fils per day was quite an attraction. Going to the movies at that time cost forty fils. Fifty fils was a dream.

But I declined his offer. He insisted, saying, "I need a clever boy such as you. You understand things quickly. You can look over the accounts, see where the money goes. You're not like that jackass, Hazim."

I could see that he was kidding his son. The word jackass didn't shock me the way it had the first time. I turned to Hazim and saw him laughing.

I kept on going to see Mary and her mother. Something drew me to their house. I needed a miracle to control myself and stop my tears.

Madeleine was not a woman who could simply be forgotten. She was like Selam, holding a quiet place deep in my heart. I saw how the catastrophe had affected Madeleine's mother. A pallor perfused her face. She was dressed in black, the same as Mary.

She told me that a man from Alqush had asked for Mary's hand in marriage. This man's sister was their neighbor, and he was staying with her. He was widowed and had two small children.

Mary had refused his proposal. She wanted an educated man from Mosul. We called such men *effendi*. Mary's mother asked me, "Where will she find an *effendi*?"

I told her that Mary knew her own interests. Her mother's eyes filled with tears. "If she knows her own interests, why did she refuse him?"

Mary said, "That wasn't the reason. I wouldn't mind marrying him, and I wouldn't mind raising his children. But I can't live in a village. If he comes here and finds work here, I'll marry him. But he wore out the leather in his shoes and couldn't find a job."

Her mother gasped with dismay, but didn't say anything.

I asked her, "What work does he do?"

"He's a carpenter. There are already plenty of excellent carpenters here. Ordinary people in the village will buy anything, but here, the furniture has to be good."

"Is he smart?"

"Yes. Very sharp."

"If he's smart enough I can find a job for him with a good carpenter here in Mosul. I know someone who's looking for a reliable man."

Mary's mother cried, "You can do that?" She could hardly believe her ears. "Do it now. Tomorrow. Anytime. I'll go get him." She rushed out of the house without her cloak.

Shortly after that, a young man appeared at the door. He was in his early thirties, red-haired and handsome. He asked Mary about me. She pointed to me. From the look on his face I could see that he doubted that a child could solve a complex problem like finding him work.

I asked him, "Are you ready to go right now?"

"Yes."

We talked on the way to Hazim's father's shop. I found out his name was Jameel. He knew his future lay in the city, and I could see he was clever and ambitious.

He told me, "If a carpenter is good at his profession, it doesn't matter to me if he pays me less than I deserve. I'll learn the profession from him and then I'll stand on my own feet."

When we drew near "Carpentry of the Future" I said to him, "Stay here, let me talk to him first. If he doesn't hire you, you won't feel embarrassed." Abu Hazim was praying the afternoon prayer on a carpet surrounded by piles of sawdust. When he bowed and prostrated himself, the soft sawdust flew in all directions.

Neither Hazim nor the workers were there. Abu Hazim smiled when he saw me. "Did you change your mind?"

I said, "Yes and no."

He laughed, "I'm puzzled."

"I brought you a carpenter from Alqush. You only have to tell him something once. He'll learn fast and become very skilled."

"Bring him in."

They agreed that Jameel would begin work the next day. Abu Hazim appeared very comfortable with Jameel, more so than I expected. He promised to give him a raise if he made a good effort.

A month later Jameel married Mary. I was the guest of honor at the wedding. It was the first time I had ever entered a church.

The priest recited the ritual, sometimes in Aramaic and at other times in Arabic. I was intrigued as the priest recited the conditions of marriage, such as the obligation of fidelity in health and disease, poverty and wealth, and so forth, because they were new to me.

I understood some Aramaic words from before I went to school, but I had since forgotten them all, along with my Turkmen, Kurdish, and Hebrew. I had forgotten them when I started reading and writing in Arabic.

Because of the atmosphere of the church, the grandeur of the place, and the solemnity of the marriage ceremony, I thought the parties would be sure to be faithful to each other. Three years later, I read the Kinsey report about infidelity in the United States in a series written for *Helmi Murad*. It shook the image of what I had heard in the church.

After the marriage, for reasons that I didn't understand, I suppressed several times my strong desire to visit Mary and her mother. And I didn't go to the furniture shop, so I didn't see Hazim, Jameel, or Hazim's father. I stayed away from them all for more than a month.

The first time I visited them after that, I saw a house filled with happiness. Jameel's two daughters, a two-year-old and a four-year-old, were beautiful. After a few minutes of shyness they started playing with me. I noticed that marriage had had an effect on Mary. Her face was radiant with happiness and contentment.

But I noticed that her mother, alone, was suffering deeply, though she tried to mask it with a smile.

I don't know how I was able to read the future. I felt in my heart that she wouldn't live long after that, and what I expected came true. Madeleine and Mary's mother died in less than six months. Coming on top of the loss of my beautiful Madeleine, this hurt me deeply again.

I had become good friends with Qazi, the son of a famous lawyer, and his cousin. They had been my classmates in the eighth grade. Qazi's uncle had a food shop in a busy part of Mosul, quite close to Mary's house. Standing in front of the shop I could see the street that Mary's house was on. I remembered Madeleine and how her eyes shone the last time I saw her. I remembered her hands clutching at mine. The pain stabbed my heart again.

I used to linger in front of the store sometimes before going home. One winter day, I was standing with Qazi, when the man who sold sugar-coated almonds passed in front of us. Qazi bought a quarter kilogram. He put half of them in a small bag and gave them to me.

When I put a piece in my mouth, I remembered Jameel's two daughters. I told Qazi, "I'm sorry, I have to leave." I rushed to Mary's house with the hot almonds in my hand.

The door was ajar, and when I opened it I saw Mary at her usual place, behind a German Pfaf sewing machine. Now that she was married, she was no longer exposing her black hair. She wore a beautiful colored scarf which covered her hair and the top of her forehead. She looked younger than she had before. She had gotten a little heavier. The extra weight made her chin more prominent and made her even more beautiful.

She didn't recognize me at first. I had disappeared for more than a year. Then she cried, straight from her heart, "Oh, you forgot all about your good friends, you traitor! Where did you disappear to? I hardly recognize you. You've grown. Come in."

I approached her and at the same time I could hear children's noises coming from Madeleine's room. When I got near Mary she pulled me close in a tight, affectionate hug. She kissed me on my cheek and forehead. Before I said anything I gave her the bag of almonds. She took one and put it in her mouth. She cried, "It's hot, you imp, you tricked me."

I whispered in her ear, "Have you had a baby?" She pointed to Madeleine's room. I hurried over, opened the door, and saw Jameel's two beautiful daughters playing with a baby lying on his back, a few months old, waving his hands and feet. With the girls on either side of him, he was laughing constantly, his voice like music. He was pale with black hair, just like Mary. But his features were his father's.

I sat nearby and gave them the almonds. I divided them equally between them. There was one left, so I put it in my mouth.

Mary's words from a long time before remained in my ears: "Would you eat from a bowl of yogurt after the skin is broken?"

The tradition at the time, and I don't know if it still holds, was that a person had a bowl of yogurt to himself, and the one who broke the skin ate the whole thing. If he left it, no one else would eat it, because it wasn't his.

I didn't understand what she meant. The only thought I had at the time was that Diya', by rejecting Madeleine's love, had destroyed his own honor and Madeleine's pride. She had killed herself in this painful way, though I believed fervently that there were any number of young men who would have married her. And though I understood her behavior and what drove her to it, I thought there was no excuse for it. But the enigma of Mary's words, along with my affection for her, made me waver in my judgment of Madeleine.

Madeleine opened the door to my appreciation of female beauty. If Madeleine had not come into my life, that door would have remained closed until some years later. That early discovery established in me a taste for the wonders of the body, if only from a distance, and brought me nearer to an understanding of human sexuality.

I was not capable of understanding adult reality. And telling adults what had happened and asking what they thought would have been to betray Madeleine's secrets. And that I could not bear. I could only guess. It was only when I was in my twenties that I understood the secret of what happened to her. The skin of the yogurt symbolized the hymen. Breaking the skin meant eating the whole yogurt. And nobody would want to eat a contaminated yogurt with a broken skin. Madeleine gave her virginity to her beloved, and he betrayed her. He broke her and left her no hope in life.

Madeleine wasn't like other girls. She was a beacon of beauty and love and a provocation, proud of her beauty and her gifts and eager to bestow them on others. And so Diya''s treachery had to be met with a harsh punishment of herself, even if it meant her death. She was outstanding in all things, and she had to be outstanding in her death.

That was the last time I saw Mary. Selam and Madeleine had left wounds in my heart. No one can control memories, or when they appear and when they disappear. Countless times their image has appeared to me suddenly, plunging me into a deep sadness, overwhelming me. Even after decades of marriage my wife often catches me and asks, "Why are you so sad?" I look at her numbly and don't know how to reply. I have tried to forget them, in vain.

When I met Adnan the genius a few years later, I understood his indignation with the entire universe. He had lost his father in Palestine and then he had lost his mother months after that.

He was full of rebellion against everything. He used to say, "If God is capable of mercy, why he didn't help my parents? And if God isn't capable of help or compassion, why should we worship him? We have no need of a useless God."

I understood him, but my pain didn't lessen. Our pain and joy, our victories and defeats, remain with us until death.

PART SIX

To Love Anew

Sami would join me whenever I passed by my father's store. I liked him because he would tell me about the strange and enthralling world of the movies. He enjoyed my company because I helped him make toy cars from pieces of wire and listened to him without interrupting. He would sometimes ask me to read what was written on the pictures because he couldn't read or write. I was surprised that his father didn't badger him about that, but I later learned that he had done well at the synagogue and had learned to read and write in Hebrew. As for Arabic, it was left up to him whether to learn it or not, and if he didn't want to, that was his business. Arabic for him was for worldly things, for talking, buying, and selling; while Hebrew was for the reading of the Torah at the synagogue. Language is what separates religion from worldly things. Sami didn't need to learn Arabic writing because he was going to take over his father's store, like all the other sons of Muslim, Jewish, and Christian shop owners.

The customers in the market were mostly Arab, Turkmen, Kurdish, Aramaean, Assyrian, Yazidi, and Jewish villagers. By working at my father's and brother's stores, I had learned a few words of each of their languages, but I forgot them all after I started school. On the first day of school, I told Sami that I could write in Arabic. He had tried before to teach me how to write my name in Hebrew, but I wasn't interested. I started to write my name for him, but before I finished, my father returned from the mosque and asked me to bring down a bundle of baskets from storage. Sami went with me, and we passed by Hamu, who had a copy of *Akhir Sa'a* and was looking at a picture of a young woman with a one-piece bathing suit on the beach in Alexandria. She was smiling as she stood with her back to the Mediterranean Sea. The caption read: *Bye-bye my love, until we meet again next summer.*

Hamu was seated on the steps that led to the storage. When he saw me looking at the picture he said, "Can you read what it says about the picture?"

I read the caption. His eyes brightened and he said, "After you take the baskets to your dad, come back and read to me." Sami and I were very eager, but I wasn't able to return because I was given another chore to do.

In the summer Sami would accompany me to the river, where I would soak the baskets. The temperature in the shade would be 115 to 125 degrees Fahrenheit. Baskets, fans, and brooms would dry up and begin to shatter from the heat. The basket weavers would stack ten to a bundle, one inside the other. The dry baskets were light and easy to carry, but when they were wet their weight would double or even quadruple. The water would drip on us as we walked, but the baskets would be dry by the time we reached the store. Sami used to help me pull the baskets out of the water. He was careful, though, to have his dishdasha dry before returning to his father, who would yell at him for being careless. I told Sami about the beautiful pictures that hung in the restaurants, and asked if he would like to come with me to see them the next day.

The next day he went with me to the Al-Thoub Café on the Tigris River. He was less impressed than I had been. He said that movies were more amazing than mere still pictures. He had talked so much about the movies that I had begun to dream of going. I used to look at the movie posters on either side of the entrance to Bab Al-Toub. The beauty of the pictures delighted me, as did the artful calligraphy, but I would never think of entering the theater. Going to the theater would mean getting my father's approval, which was virtually impossible. But my dream came true in the summer after my first year in school. Ramadan and the Eid occurred in summer that year, and my friend Ghanem, who was related to the husband of my older sister Wahiba, said, "We don't need our parents' permission during the Eid. In the Eid everything is allowed, but once the Eid is over things will get back to normal."

Sami was "unhurried" about education, as his father, our neighbor in the Atami market, would say. His usual response to Sami's progress in school was "Sami is fast in everything, but unhurried at school."

Sami was twelve years old, like me. We were both registered at school during the same year, but Sami took two years to complete each grade. He miraculously passed the third grade test, and an elaborate party, to which I was invited, was held in his honor. To my dismay I couldn't attend. Children couldn't go out at night—even for a few minutes—without the accompaniment of an adult, and his house was too far from mine. Laughing, Sami described the party to me, adding to my disappointment. He told me how the party began at dusk and went all night.

There was now a two-year gap between us at school. Sami didn't care that he couldn't read or write anything that wasn't part of his assigned homework. I never thought of him as inferior to me. He was very intelligent in all subjects that didn't relate to school, and brilliant at creating what he needed. He once carved a magnificent pistol—the object of my bottomless admiration—out of plywood, painted it black, and carried it in his belt as he re-created for me the stories of adventure films and cowboy movies. I stood in awe of the way he narrated these stories and his ability to act out all the roles, especially the hero's. He would expertly draw the gun from his belt and shout "Hands up!" while firing a few bullets to finish off his enemies. Listening to him, hanging on his every word, I would picture the fallen victims and his indifference toward them. In the summer we would often flee the noisy and congested market, ascend the stairs, and sit in the wholesalers' center between our fathers' small warehouses, a quiet space where there were no customers or businessmen. Sami would fill the emptiness with his stories. He was the story-teller, the speaker, and the actor; and I was the starry-eyed listener.

The Public Education Ministry had designated "The Hall of the Chaste" a testing site for the sixth grade baccalaureate, which used to be called the ministerial test. The Hall of the Chaste was a very large hall in the School of Our Virgin Lady. The school was about a twenty-minute walk away, in a quarter which ran from the Tigris in the east to the outskirts of the city in the west. The Jews occupied most of the northern sector, the Christians lived in the west and the rest of the northern part, and the Moslems occupied the remaining neighborhoods and streets, rubbing elbows with both communities.

The first day of testing went very well. I was done and out of the great Hall of the Chaste within an hour. I found a handful of students from other schools, whom I had never met before, gathered in the hallway. They ran up to me and asked how I had answered some of the questions. They told me their answers, and I told them mine. We spent some time discussing what we thought were the correct answers. Suddenly I felt two hands covering my eyes and a voice said: "Guess who?"

The last person I expected was Sami. He had told me where his house was, but I had never been there. It was at least a twenty-minute walk—walking fast—from my house, and quite far from where I worked in the summer. It never occurred to me that his house was close to the Hall of the Chaste, where I was taking the ministerial test. Instead of teasing me by asking again, he hopped around and appeared in front of me, a complete surprise. Laughing, he cried out, "Who did you say?"

My heart was gladdened to see him. "How did you know I was here?"

"We all knew you'd be taking the test. There aren't that many sites for the ministerial tests, and your school's near here." He tugged on my arm and said: "Let's go home. The food's ready."

It was a little past nine in the morning. "I can't, I'm not hungry. I never eat before noon."

"Fine, don't eat. My mother wants to see you." We had only taken a few steps when a young girl ran up to us, like a tempest. She was younger than we were, perhaps ten years old; shorter than Sami; and brown-skinned with pretty features and brilliant, joyful black eyes and dark chestnut hair. She looked a lot like Sami, but was much thinner, as thin as Selam. I later found out that her name was Sumaya. She called my name and hugged me as if she had known me all her life. She pulled me by the hand toward their home. I had to follow her while talking to Sami, who was holding on to my left hand. Together they pulled me home. The young girl skipped along as if dancing. Sami and I laughed. As we approached the house, we saw their mother waiting at the door. In accordance with custom she was called Umm Salim (Mother of Salim, her eldest son). She looked to be a few years younger than my mother. She didn't look at all like her children. She was a heavy, brown-skinned woman with hair pulled back by a *biyazma,* the silken headscarf worn by women. Hers was red, while my mother and my women relatives preferred theirs to be black. Her style was more modern than my mother's, more like my older married sister's. She greeted me joyously, gave me a strong hug and a kiss on the cheek, and then pulled me inside the house.

Their house was much better than ours. It had many rooms, and it was all marble, even the courtyard. The courtyard was about ten meters square, and in the middle of it was a small garden about two meters across, surrounded by a foot-high wall of blue marble covered with wild roses of varied colors. Our courtyard was made of cement, while theirs was tiled with a brilliant light-blue marble. Our house had no marble except for the two bedroom door handles. There was bedding spread out in each of the rooms, while at home we all slept on the floor.

Hasqail depended, as did many Jews in our market, on loaning money to the Jewish and Kurdish farmers outside of Mosul, where many Kurds, Jews, Assyrians, Syriacs, Yazidis, and Turkmen farmers lived. This gave him a sufficient income to live comfortably. And so Hasqail didn't depend on the store's income, and his store was almost empty of goods.

When I think about that situation now, I imagine that Hasqail, Mukhlif, and others used the store as a negotiating center, a meeting place for the farmers, not a place for selling like my father's store. That practice was common in our poor city, in which sources of income were scarce, in contrast to Baghdad with its crowds of workers; Basra with its large port, oil companies, and prolific date crops; or Kirkuk, which was considered the most important source of petroleum in Iraq.

Sami's mother said, "If you only knew the headache Sami has given us! He's been waiting since the test started. He said you'd leave early. Come, come here." We went into a small kitchen, where a small round table about a foot off the ground was set with plates of cream, honey, bread, cheese, and other food, and surrounded by several small seats. "Now please, help yourself."

"I can't eat, I ate just a while ago," I apologized. I really was full; we weren't used to eating between meals.

"Tea, then?"

"That will be fine."

"How were your answers?"

"I don't know."

Umm Salim laughed. "Sami says you'll be first."

I was embarrassed, not knowing how to reply.

Sami said, "I told you, wait till the results are out. You'll see."

I said nothing. She tenderly patted my head and said, "You'll do just fine. I can see it in your eyes."

We then went to a small room near the front door, which I hadn't noticed before. Sami opened its door, and there were dozens of tools, arranged in an easily accessible way, that were used to fix whatever got broken in the house: hammers, scissors of all sizes and kinds, screwdrivers, and saws of all sizes. One of them was for wood, and I thought that must be how Sami had made the detailed pistol I had dreamed of buying. I hadn't been able to save enough money for it, as my daily wages had been raised to ten fils only a short while before. But I had learned from Sami how to make different kinds of cars from various lengths of wire. He had learned from his brother Salim, who had shown him the right tools to use.

"Stay with us," Sami said, and his mother and Sumaya joined him. Sumaya never let go of my hand. She hung on to me with an affection I couldn't fathom.

I apologized. "I can't. Tomorrow is the English test, and I have to review."

They let me go. Sami and Sumaya were waiting for me, however, every day at the door. I would spend about a quarter of an hour with them, drink tea, walk around the neighborhood, and then return home. On the day before the final test, my father surprised me by saying, "Why do you refuse to eat at Sami's house?"

I was embarrassed; I didn't know what to say. Some of my school friends used to say that the Jews killed children and used their blood in religious ceremonies; however, the fact that my father, a religious man, would allow me to eat at their house meant that these stories had to be lies. And so after I finished the test I went sprinting off with Sami and Sumaya toward their house, in complete happiness.

We went to Sami, Sumaya, and Salim's bedroom. There were three beds, and in the middle there was a small circular area with cushions where we sat. Sami immediately brought wires, pliers, clips, and an iron pipe about an inch in diameter that we wrapped wires around in order to make wheels for the car. Sami's mother would look in on us every once in a while and smile. Late in the afternoon she brought us lemon juice with sugar and surprised me by saying, "You'll spend the night with us."

Startled, I said, "No, I haven't told my parents."

"They won't worry. Abu Salim told your father and he agreed."

As soon as Sami and Sumaya heard that they cheered, "Hooray!" Sumaya grabbed me and kissed me, in front of her mother and brother. I was overcome with embarrassment. I felt the blood burn in my cheeks, and I broke out in a sweat. Their mother must have sensed that because she left, and we went on playing.

Umm Salim's eyes showed the deep respect she had for me. This was not just because of my friendship to Sami, but because I had once done something that had earned the respect of all the Jews.

More than a year before, Sami and I had been playing with the wire cars in the Khan Al-Bazazeen neighborhood. Sami would make the cars at home, and then bring them to me on summer days so I could finish some of the work with him whenever I wasn't too busy with errands for my father or the Mad Dog. It wasn't often that I could steal a few moments to play with Sami. The cars he made were very beautiful. On that day the car had a shaft, about an arm's length, made up of several twisted wires that ended in a steering wheel that controlled the car's direction, left or right. All the children around our age were jealous. On that day Sa'doun, the son of one of the shop owners whose store was at the entrance to the market, could no longer restrain himself from wanting to play with our toys. He pushed Sami down, snatched the car, and ran away. Sami ran after him and grabbed onto his dishdasha, causing Sa'doun to lose his balance, fall to the ground, and cut his head. Blood flowed everywhere—I don't know why children's blood is so abundant! Sami took the car and ran back to his father's store. He scurried to the back of the store as fast as lightning and hid, not telling his father what had happened.

Abdullah, Sa'doun's father, came holding his son's hand, with blood still flowing over Sa'doun's face. He started screaming in Hasqail's face, "With these two hands I'll take your son to police headquarters!" Hasqail's face went pale. People gathered, drawn by the shouting, and were moved by the sight of blood flowing from Sa'doun's forehead. The whispers rose: "A Jew did that to a Muslim." Hasqail didn't say a word. His face was the color of turmeric.

I was at my father's store, waiting for him to return from the noon prayer at the Aghwat Mosque. He showed up a few minutes later as the crowd and noise were getting serious. When Abdullah saw him he said, "Are you going to allow this, you the Mullah? Are you going to let a Jew do this to my son?" Before my father could respond, I shouted, "It's Sa'doun's fault! He stole Sami's carriage—Sami didn't want to hurt him, he just wanted his carriage back. He grabbed Sa'doun's dishdasha and Sa'doun fell and cut his forehead!"

The noise calmed immediately. Abdullah looked at his son angrily. Like a man possessed, he screamed, "You stole the carriage?"

Sa'doun didn't reply, lowering his head in embarrassment. His father raised his hand to hit him. "You deserve more than a cut on the head. I ought to kill you, you miserable pup."

My father grasped Abdullah's hand and said, "Don't be angry, they're just kids."

"Let me discipline him. He shamed me in front of the whole market. He embarrassed me, the dog."

But my father told him gravely, "First hurry and treat his cut, and when he's well, do as you see fit."

The people who had gathered laughed and went on their way. As soon as the crowd had left, a panting policeman showed up, walking so fast he was almost running. He stopped in front of Hasqail's store, looked at my father, and asked, "Where's the victim?"

My father smiled, and Abu Mohammad, the owner of the shop next door, said "Go back, there's no victim. Nobody got hurt."

That incident made my reputation among the Jews. I became their spoiled child. Sometimes when it was very hot, and walking in the sun was torture, I would, with my father's permission, get away from the Mad Dog and take a nap at Mukhlif the Jew's store. Mukhlif loved me greatly. He would spread a piece of cloth on the wide store floor for me to sleep on, right under the ceiling fan, and place a roll of cloth under my head. I would sleep as soon as my head touched the roll. This was special, a treatment no one else got.

My mother didn't cook lunch. We usually had a light lunch, and dinner was our main meal. Umm Salim, I noticed, prepared lunch as the main meal. She gave us rice, gravy, and *shinin*— yogurt diluted with water—with radishes and green onions. That was the heaviest lunch I had ever had on a regular day since childhood. Like the majority of poor and middle-class people in Iraq, we didn't eat rice except on holidays and during the month of Ramadan.

Sumaya didn't eat much. Her mother tried to make her eat more, but to no avail. So she brought her a teacup with a red liquid in it and begged her to drink it, but Sumaya shook her head, and so Umm Salim pointed to me and said threateningly, "If you don't drink this, he'll get upset and go home."

Sumaya was attached to me, and she looked into my eyes and said, "Will you really leave?"

"Yes, if you don't drink the medicine."

She smiled and said, "It's not medicine, it's juice."

I was embarrassed. Her mother said, "Yes, it's good juice."

She took it and drank it in one gulp, and in a few minutes she began to eat, little by little.

After lunch Sami's mother asked us to take a nap. We went into the children's bedroom. Sami's mother changed the covers on Salim's bed, then left and shut the door behind her. I lay on Salim's bed; Sami lay on the bed across from it. I could see him and converse with him, while Sumaya was standing next to me still holding my hand.

I asked Sami, "When will Salim get back from the movies?"

"He's not working at the movies anymore. He won't be back. He's traveling.

"To Baghdad?" It was the first name that came to me, because I had always heard about people traveling to Baghdad.

"I don't know."

"They didn't tell you where he went?"

"They said it's a long way away."

"When will he be back?"

"I don't know. I wish he hadn't left."

"Why?"

"Don't you know?"

I shook my head. "No."

"Who's going to take me to the movies?"

The girl laughed and said, "I will."

We were getting sleepy and yet we continued to talk happily. I was almost asleep when Sumaya awakened me by jumping onto my bed and sitting on the pillow by my head. She laughed and said, "Close your eyes, I'll let you sleep on my arm."

I closed my eyes, and she started stroking my hair. She said, "You have coarse hair. Sami's hair is soft." I always shaved my head with a number one razor, keeping my hair shorter than a centimeter, because I had nosebleeds. Perhaps that's why my hair is coarse. Sumaya's touch was like balsam. I must have fallen asleep, because suddenly the mother was waking us up and lifting Sumaya from my side. She had fallen asleep on the pillow, her head falling onto my stomach.

Later, we ran around in the garden, stopping whenever one of us would say a certain word. I don't know how the evening fell on us so fast. That was one of the happiest days of my life. I was freed from the Mad Dog, playing with a happiness I had never dreamed of. After a while Hasqail came. A while later a few families began to arrive, without their children. There were women, young ladies, young men, and older men; each carrying fruits, vegetables, other food, or a bottle, juice drinks, or arak. The young men were busy bringing in chairs from the neighbors; there were at least twenty chairs arranged in a circle around the small garden. Other men came that I recognized from the market. But my friend Mukhlif, whom I loved more than all of them, was not among them. Then came some young men carrying musical instruments: a lute, violin, fiddle, drums, and a flute. I had seen drums and flutes being sold at Bab Al-Toub, but the violin and fiddle I had never seen before.

The newcomers were heartily greeted by all as the comments, jokes, and laughter grew louder. The women were gathered near the kitchen or in it. Some of them sat on the folding chairs that they had brought with them. And soon the smell of food was overwhelming. We were playing the *muhaibis* game in the children's room. We would place a towel over someone's hands while they held a bead, then take the towel away and try to guess which hand held the bead. After a while Hasqail called Sami. Sumaya said seriously, "Now we'll have to play alone. Sami's going to work."

"What work?"

"Don't you know? Didn't he tell you?"

"No, he didn't tell me."

"He's a '*boy*.'"

It was the first time I had ever heard that word. I stared at her, and she said, "Sami's going to wait on people. Then they'll pass the hat and give him a hundred fils."

I laughed. "That's a real fortune."

"Yes. Would you agree to work for that much?"

"No."

"Me neither. It's very tiring."

And truly Sami's job was very tiring; they all sat around the circular garden, almost twenty-five people, Sami running between them passing out the arak bottles and juice drinks, the cups, and the *mezze,* the appetizers. Those close to the garden would place their cups and plates on the low wall. Those farther away had small tables next to them. There were two small tables in front of the musicians that had all they needed to eat or drink. They began to play popular local and Egyptian songs. Sumaya stopped playing with me, then stood in the doorway and started dancing to the music. All the men looked at her and clapped to encourage her. The women started laughing and clapping too. A buxom young woman with light chestnut hair, almost blond, started dancing in front of Sumaya, smiling. They were a great pair. I noticed that Sami's mother would smile, wipe a tear, and disappear into the kitchen. Her tears pierced my heart.

Sumaya and her beautiful companion danced for several minutes, until Sumaya got tired. When she stopped dancing the young woman lifted her and started kissing her and laughing. Sumaya left the young woman and returned to sit by me. She hugged me, panting from her dancing.

The whole gathering was watching Zahi, a thin, dark, clean-shaven young man with a long tapering chin, full lips, and wide eyes. They begged him to start, but he ignored their pleas. He was drinking his arak slowly and savoring the chicken, salad, hyacinth beans, and broad beans like a gourmet, joking and laughing heartily. At eight o'clock he raised his hand and signaled to the musicians to start. Everyone, men and women, clapped fervently.

He started by strumming a beautiful solo on the lute that won everyone's approval; many were shouting: "Allah, Allah." He then played another solo on the violin, an old Iraqi song that the radio orchestra often played. Meanwhile the flute plumbed the depths, rousing buried sorrows and submerged pain. The women wiped their tears. But Zahi soon stopped. He picked up the *qanoun,* a stringed instrument resembling the zither, and made it hover in a forest paradise where magical nightingales migrated. Sumaya and I were seated on the door step, and Umm Salim would every once in a while bring us something to eat: hyacinth beans, pomegranates, peas, and peeled carrots. She would bring the food in a small bowl with two spoons, one for the beans and one for the pomegranates. But Sumaya forbade me to use my spoon; she insisted, "One spoon is enough."

She fed me, but would not allow me to feed her. And when her mother brought the steamy legumes, she would peel them, take a bite, and place the rest into my mouth. I was embarrassed, because I could see that some of the women were watching Sumaya sadly; they would wipe tears from their eyes, then turn their backs to us. But Sumaya persisted.

Zahi's deep, warm voice dominated the gathering, causing the audience to applaud and call for him to repeat stanza after stanza. Zahi had perfected the delivery of the Iraqi *maqam,* a traditional song form. I was an innocent child; I didn't like *maqam.*

I preferred Egyptian songs, but that night Zahi opened my mind and I learned to appreciate and love *maqam*. While before I used to turn the radio off as soon as I heard a *maqam*, since that night, whenever I hear these songs, I stop and find out who the singer is and what he is singing.

Almost thirty years later, in the early seventies, I heard Zahi's name on the Al-Quds radio station. He was leading an Iraqi musical group in *maqam* songs. Recalling that special evening in my childhood, I moved closer to the radio, and luckily he played some of the songs he had sung that night, songs I have never forgotten.

Sumaya asked me, "Would you like some *sharab?*"

I had never heard of *sharab* except here at their house at noon when Sumaya had to drink it. I didn't know what it was. I asked, "Grape juice?"

She nodded. "Yes."

She jumped up as fast as lightning and half filled a cup from a bottle that had a picture of a vineyard on it. The liquid looked almost red when she added the honey and stirred it with a small spoon. She took a small sip to taste, and gave it to me. "Just a sip. Don't drink the whole thing."

I took a sip. It tasted wonderful, but it wasn't grape juice. She said, "I used to be very thin. My father took me to the doctor, and he told me to drink a cup of *sharab* with honey every day. Now I'm as healthy as a deer, don't you think?"

"Yes."

"I'm fat now."

"No, you're not fat. You're thin, thinner than me."

She cried out: "No I'm fat, my parents say so."

I gave in. "Yes, you're fat."

She looked at me: "Don't you know Asma?"

"Who's Asma?"

"My sister."

"No, I've never seen her."

"I've never seen her either."

"What's wrong with her?

"She died."

"Why?"

"Because they didn't take her to the doctor. She was thin like me. She didn't eat, and she died. If she had gone to the doctor and drunk *sharab* with honey she wouldn't have died. I would have had a sister to play with, like Rachel."

"Who's Rachel?"

"Our neighbor. She's my age. She plays with her sister all day."

"Why don't you play with them?"

"They don't come here much."

"Go to their house."

Their house is very small. We don't all fit there, so we play in the street. But my mother doesn't let me play in the street. The street's dirty. If Asma had lived, she'd be older than Sami."

"Then she might not play with you."

"Why?"

"Older kids don't play. They study, they read, and they do house work."

She smiled and wrapped her thin arms around my neck. "I'd force her to play with me. I'd cut her hair while she slept if she didn't play with me."

I laughed. "She'd hit you when she woke up."

She moved away from me, stared into my eyes, and said: "No one can hit me."

"Why?"

"Because I'm weak. They let me do what I please. They're scared for me."

"All right, then."

She grabbed my hand, I rose, and she dragged me into the room. She said, "Sit on the bed." I obeyed. She opened my arms, and stood in between them, close to the bed.

"Open your mouth." I opened my mouth. She said, "Leave it open," and I did. She put a teaspoon of the *sharab* in her mouth, and then she put her tongue in my mouth and started moving it around in my mouth.

Some of the *sharab* went to my stomach. She drew back and asked me, "It's good, isn't it?"

I laughed and said, "No."

"Why not?"

"I don't know. I'd prefer it if you would use a teaspoon and not your tongue."

"All right, open your mouth." She put a teaspoonful in my mouth and another in her mouth, and then kissed me on the mouth, and asked, "What about now?"

"Yes, it's good."

By the time we finished the *sharab*, I had lost control of myself; I didn't know what was happening to me. My body temperature had risen and I had no resistance. She pulled me again to the doorstep in front of the musicians and the crowd of men. I followed her orders meekly. She sat in my lap and threw her thin arm around my neck, then leaned her head next to my face, her breath on my cheek. A comfortable numbness crept into my blood that allowed me to sink into the music and singing, the cigarette smoke, and the happiness and laughter. I was almost limp; I leaned my head against the marble door frame. I am sure Sumaya must have been feeling the same way; she got even closer to me. I no longer cared about the sad way in which the women were looking at us, a sadness I didn't understand, nor did I understand some of their tears, especially since everyone was happy with Zahi's songs and his beautiful voice, and the whole world was suffused with a heavenly air of beauty and magic.

The men were smoking, clapping, and swaying, enchanted by music and drink; and Zahi was strumming and singing to the glorious bright stars. The women were seated by the kitchen; once in a while one of them would get up to check on the food she was cooking. A thick, enticing aroma came through the kitchen door and two small windows to tease our hunger. The smells were mixed: fried onions with spices, stewed and roasted meat, and boiled rice mingled with the smells from the men's corner, arak and cigarettes.

While I was sitting there in a stupor, I was startled by a young woman about the same age as the ravishing Madeleine, though not quite as beautiful. She had rosy cheeks, olive skin, dark brown hair, full lips, a green satin blouse open a long way down toward her prominent breasts, and a red striped skirt over a figure that was full without any hint of being fat.

She wore a chain culminating in a gold moon halo that hung between her breasts. She had a beautiful smile and large eyes. She stooped to caress Sumaya's cheek, then pointed to me and said, "Do you love him?"

Sumaya nodded and tightened her grip on my neck. The young woman laughed and passed her fingers through my hair. I felt a tremendous warmth which I had never felt before. She asked, "Do you love her?"

My ears and face burned. Sumaya squeezed me and said confidently, "Yes, he loves me."

The young woman looked at me, smiling, and said, "What about me, don't you love me?"

My embarrassment increased. She went on caressing my hair, face, ear, and neck, arousing and enslaving me further. I no longer knew what to say; I wished I were somewhere else.

She kissed Sumaya's cheek, then kissed me and gently bit my cheek. I was melting. She winked, bent her head to the side and said, "What about now? Don't you love me?"

Sumaya shouted, "No, he loves me. You're too old for him."

Before she finished talking, another young woman of about the same age stooped next to her, perhaps a friend of hers. She was very pale, with light brown hair, thin crimson lips, and hazel eyes as light as her hair. Her hair, like that of Asmahan, the famous singer, was parted in the middle and lay in beautiful curls. She had an elongated face with a sharp chin and pretty features—very attractive— and wore a flaring silk skirt striped in black, blue, white, and red, and a red blouse, revealing two lovely white arms. When she raised her arm I could see curly black hair under it that was strangely arousing. She seemed to come from a rich family; she was decorated with more golden jewelry than I would have thought possible. She wore a golden necklace decorated with walnut-sized gold roses that fell onto her breasts, and more than twenty bracelets on each arm. She must have been enchanted by the musical sound of the bracelets on her arms, because she constantly moved them. On her right ring finger she had a shining ring topped by a precious blue stone. I can still see it now, more than half a century later: a diamond—I think—though I can't estimate its value because I don't know what kind it was. When she stooped next to the first young woman, she looked at Sumaya and inquired in a sweet, exaggeratedly coquettish voice, "What did he say to you?"

The first one pretended to be suffering: "Would you believe it, he doesn't love me."

The second young woman placed her palms under my face and Sumaya's. "Let her be. Look at me. I love you, do you love me?"

"Yes," cried Sumaya, but I couldn't say a word, I was so embarrassed. I lowered my head. She opened two buttons on my shirt and placed her hand on my chest and began to caress my nipples in a very skillful and exciting way. I was overcome with excitement and pleasure, and I laughed wholeheartedly. She asked, "Will you marry me?"

The first young woman smiled, and I was embarrassed again. The other kissed me, went back to playing with my chest, and repeated, "Tell me. Will you marry me?"

I was struck dumb with arousal, bathed in sweat.

Sumaya shouted: "No, I will marry him. Don't be jealous."

"Sumaya, do you love me? I'm your friend. I love you."

"Yes, I love you."

"Then he'll marry both of us. What do you say?"

Sumaya thought for a few moments, but before she could answer, a number of girls her age or a little older came to our side. They began to caress us, play with our hair, and kiss us. Sumaya was disturbed and cried out, "I'm the one who's going to marry him. All of you get out of here!"

They all laughed, and before the first two young women rose from our side, they kissed us both several times.

Suddenly the band began to play the dance music that accompanies Iraqi *basta* dancing songs. All the men got up and moved their chairs, making room for a circle in the middle. An attractive young dark-complexioned woman went to the center of the circle. She had a shawl tied around her waist and started shaking her belly, like Tahiya Karioka or Samia Jamal. Everyone clapped fervently. All the women came from the kitchen and stood around the music circle and clapped. As soon as the first *basta* ended, Zahi began another one. The first dancer left and another young woman took her place. The dancing peaked when the sixth dancer, a slender and graceful young woman with plain features, began to dance.

She had long, straight black hair that fell to her hips, and she wore an elegant white blouse that stopped short of her navel, while her skirt reached the ground. She had a scarf tied around her hips, and as she danced she bent till her hair brushed the ground. The pure white skin around her navel was magically alluring, provocative in its youthful vigor. I was not yet twelve years of age, and I thought she was not human. She was a radiant light dissolving into music, coalescing in the form of an ordinary being and then dispersing its atoms to perish in the world's eternity, only to return once again as a real being. She would dissolve with each and every rhythm, and gather with another in the dialectic of the beginning and the end, birth and dissolution, where death and life dissolve and merge again in an eternal mist that carries its constant contradiction. What great pleasure, and what torture . . .

She was the first dancer I had ever seen, and I was lost in the magic of her long hair that brushed the ground as she bent backwards. When I imagine her, my heart beats with fear that she will fall to the ground. The only other place where I ever saw dancing like that was in Morocco. Almost seventeen years later, a dancer named Shaykha would do that while she was intoxicated with alcohol, hashish, and love. And I saw a third example in an Iraqi gypsy, who had the same effect on me, in the mid-seventies. Afterward I grew old, and I stopped going to watch this toxic art—I died while still alive.

At that point Sumaya pulled at my hand and said: "Let's dance."

I went with her. She began to move her belly and hips skillfully, while I stood in front of her, stiff and embarrassed, not knowing what to do. The young women saved me. They all surrounded us, and I withdrew to the steps where I had been sitting. Sumaya went on dancing, and everyone was clapping. Even the men came to watch. Her mother gave her a hug, lifted her, and began to kiss her, saying tenderly, "That's enough, my love, don't tire yourself."

She wriggled out of her mother's arms and came and sat on my lap. I felt a great happiness, as if I were in a long and wonderful dream. It ended when I felt drops of cold water on my face. I opened my eyes to the sound of music, and Sami was sprinkling water on us, saying, "You fell asleep."

Sumaya opened her eyes too. She got off my lap and sat on the steps, with Sami next to her. I was quite comfortable, though my lap was numb. Sami asked, "Are you tired?" Their mother brought us barbecued liver and kabob, parsley with onions and sumac, warm bread, and three small bowls filled with grape juice. We were very hungry. Sumaya's cheeks had turned red, like bright wild roses. My blood was still hot, and I didn't know why. Sumaya began to feed me, and Sami laughed. He didn't stay with us long, however; someone called him, and he had to leave. I told her that if she didn't let me eat by myself I would go home. She agreed after kissing me a few times, embarrassing me again. When Sami left I felt more comfortable. I enjoyed the kisses, which burned my cheeks like the kisses of Madeleine and Selam. Once in a while, as she was kissing me, I would look in the direction of the gathering to see if anyone was watching us. Fortunately, none of the men were. The women, on the other hand, had gathered at the kitchen door, and I would notice them looking at us with a look of wonderment. Once or twice I saw one of them wipe a tear away. I didn't know what that meant.

We finished eating at about nine in the evening. Umm Salim noticed that we were sleepy, and she took us to the washroom, insisting that we wash our hands and mouths with soap, like my mother did after each meal. As soon as we were done we ran to the bedroom. I jumped onto the bed that I had napped on earlier, and Sumaya jumped on next to me.

I was worried that her mother would come and find us in the same bed and get angry. I asked her: "Why don't you sleep in your own bed?"

She answered firmly: "I like this bed better."

I closed my eyes while she kissed me and hugged my neck. I could hear the beating of her heart close to my ear. My eyelids were heavy with a sleepy ecstasy, and at the same time my fearful spirit traversed space in dread and terror, reminding me that I was alone in this world of joyful wakefulness and dreamy sleep. The atoms of my being hovered behind the tendrils of musical fire in Zahi's voice, mellow and splendid above the playing of the musicians.

Everyone else had disappeared except for Sumaya, who was attached to me, her cheek to mine, her arm around my neck, our thighs touching. My senses wavered with the blood-borne rapture that dissipated what was left of my consciousness, converting us into two lights flaring above glowing embers that burned not only skin and veins but even the bones. What remained of our bodies emitted electric currents that seared the cosmos.

That night witnessed my first step into manhood. I awakened late at night to a swelling between my legs I had never known before. I had no idea what had happened. The swelling was accompanied by great pain. I left the room. Outdoors it was empty and sad. No one was there. Where was Zahi? Where was the musical group? Where was the audience? Where were the beautiful young women? The chairs were sadly scattered in the emptiness. A small light shone above the bathroom and I had difficulty urinating. Every drop burned and brought tears to my eyes. Gradually but slowly everything returned to normal. I went back to the bedroom and lay down on Sumaya's empty bed. I fell into a deep sleep that was interrupted by someone touching my face. I opened my eyes to see Sumaya kissing me, and the light of day filled the room. She lay next to me and hugged me.

After breakfast we went to the tool room and took out the carmaking tools, even though we knew that we had passed that stage. Playing with the cars would no longer amuse us; that was all in the past. However, we made several carriages to give as gifts to the little ones.

Sami and Sumaya would not let me go home. They brought out the card deck and taught me how to play the fourteen-card *konkan* game. They taught me how to arrange the cards in my palm, and how to keep them from falling. Controlling all those cards in one hand was a challenge. We used beans for chips. Umm Salim gave each of us fifty lima beans that we placed in small bowls. Sumaya won all of our lima beans in an hour, and before we started again, Rachel and her sister came over. Sumaya cried out as she outstretched her hand and said, "This is Rachel! I told you about her." She was Sumaya's age, and her sister was almost two years older.

Other friends of Sami and Sumaya, boys and girls, also came over. It seemed that Sami had told them about me. When Sami told them my name their eyes brightened, and they competed to invite me to their homes, but Sumaya became angry and shouted "No, all of you stop."

We played until Umm Salim called us to lunch, and everyone left and we were alone again.

After a nap I taught them how to make decorations with paper and scissors. I had read about it in a book from the public library. You fold the paper in half, refold it to create four separate but equal squares, draw a design on each of the squares, and then cut it out so that when you open the paper each of these cuts shows separately. They were amused by the game, and Umm Salim liked the designs. Once they had learned the method they began to create surprisingly good designs. Sumaya designed a sheet with four squares, each containing a different size and shape design. When the sheet was opened it showed both organization and chaos. I taught her how to print the design onto a larger paper, and how to color it. She chose lilac and colored all the squares with it; it was simple and very pretty. Sami drew knives and swords, and colored them with different colors. Sumaya said, "I'll hang my picture here, above the bed."

I suddenly realized it was getting dark. I excused myself, and Sami and Sumaya accompanied me to the edge of the Jewish quarter.

I didn't dare go back that same week. I spent each morning helping my father by soaking the baskets, brooms, and fans in the Tigris, and then returning them to him. In the afternoon I would comply with the never-ending demands of the Mad Dog. I had, however, become good at wasting time by looking at the new pictures that the shop owners had cut out of the Egyptian maga-zines like *Akhir Sa'a, Al-Musawwir,* and *Al-Kawakib.* I would also read *Akhir Sa'a* and *Al-Mousawwir,* which our dear friend Hamu

Al-Hamal would bring. I used to go up to a place near my father's shop and read them. Hamu Al-Hamal brought me the magazines so that I could read the news about movie stars to him.

One afternoon a few days later, I was surprised to see Sami in the market. I greeted him with pleasure, we hugged, and he whispered, "You have to come. My mother and Sumaya want to see you."

That was in July. I didn't tell the Mad Dog, because he would have forbidden me to go. I waited until after the noon prayer, and I asked my father for permission to leave.

We went. A delicious lunch was ready, and I was hungry. There was a chicken roasted with saffron, almonds, currants and rice, and yogurt thinned with water and fruits. When Sumaya started feeding me, her mother and Sami laughed, and I was embarrassed. I had expected Salim to return from his trip, and to get angry at me when he saw Sumaya spoiling me so. He was a big man, who wouldn't have approved of such behavior from his sister. I don't know what made me look at Umm Salim and ask, "When will Salim be back?"

"He's not coming. We're going to him."

I didn't understand. "To Baghdad?"

She ignored my question and said, "We'll follow him before too long."

"All of you?"

"Yes."

"And your house?"

"We're leaving it."

"Did you sell it?"

"No, we'll just leave it."

"Why?"

She smiled but didn't answer, so I said, "What about your furniture?"

"We'll leave it here."

"But you'll need it in the new place."

"We'll buy new furniture."

"Why should you have to do that?"

"That's life."

She laughed happily, leaving me confused. Their attitude was strange, totally confusing to me at that age. We had moved from several rented houses before my father bought the small house we lived in now. Each time, we moved our furnishings and things with us. I had also seen a captain's family who moved from Baghdad and brought all their things with them on a truck that had parked not too far from the house, and the movers carried their things into the house. Why was Sami's family leaving all their things behind?

At Sami's house the siesta was strictly observed; everyone napped. Waking up afterward was very pleasant and unforgettable. We were served tea with cardamom; cookies called *kalija*, stuffed with dates, walnuts and almonds; and cakes. Afterward, Umm Salim took me to the tool room, pointed and said, "Take what you want." I didn't connect what she said with their departure from the house. I had no idea. She kept looking at me and saying, "Take what you wish."

"Do you mean I can take it home?"

"Yes."

"Why?"

"Because we're leaving it. We won't take it with us."

And once again, I could not understand. "Everything?"

"Yes."

I couldn't make anything of this. I asked again, "How can you move without your things?"

She started to laugh, and she repeated, "We'll buy new ones."

I thought for a long time and said, "Baghdad is close by, it's not far. There are trucks that move furnishings, why don't you rent one?"

She smiled, patted my head, and hugged me. She sighed and said, "I told you, take what you want."

I shook my head with a heavy heart. "I can't do that . . ." I choked; I knew I was going to cry. She bent over me and hugged me, wiped my tears, and kissed my forehead. "Don't cry. Please take what you want, as a souvenir."

I took the wood saw. I couldn't afford to buy it, and Sami was skilled with it. Along with the saw, I took some boards. On them I planned to carve several lines from the poet Raq'i and his circle, written in elegant *diwani* script. I was thinking of the stanza: *What is virtue's reward but virtue itself?*

I never dared use it, though. Every time I held the plywood I would visualize Sami, Sumaya, and their mother, and my heart would ache.

She took me to all the rooms, and pointed to everything: "Tell your mother to come tomorrow and take what she wants. Beds, wardrobes, mirrors, the bedroom set . . . You can bring a truck and take everything." I never told my mother; I never mentioned it to her. I knew she would never take anything. And even if she had agreed, there wouldn't have been any room for it in our small house.

Night came, and I told Umm Salim that I must go home. I was overcome with sadness. She kissed me again, and Sami hugged me. I looked around for Sumaya, but I didn't see her. Her mother realized that I was looking for her, and she called out, "Sumaya, where are you? He's going home." As quick as a wink, fast as lightning, she leapt from her room. She held my hand and said, "He won't leave, he's staying with us!"

I smiled, and her mother laughed: "He can't, his parents won't let him."

"Let my father go talk to them."

I laughed, and her mother stooped down and hugged her. "My love, he can't. People don't let their children sleep at their friends' houses more than once a year."

She shrieked, "But I don't want him to leave!"

I felt pressured. Sami freed my hands from her firm grip. Sumaya said, "He has to come with us. Right?"

I looked at her mother, who winked at me, and I said, "Yes, I'll go with you tomorrow."

She looked at her mother, raised her hand threateningly, and said, "If he doesn't come with us I'll stop drinking the *sharab* with honey and I'll die like my sister."

Her mother kissed her and said: "God forbid, my love. He'll come. We'll see him knocking at our door one day."

She wriggled out of her mother's arms, stood before me, and shouted, "You'll come!"

"Yes."

"I'll open the door for you."

"Yes." I turned around, walked a few steps, and heard her pull free of her mother's grasp. She threw herself on me and started crying, hugging me. "Don't leave. You'll come with us. Isn't that so? Tell the truth, you'll come."

With difficulty I pulled free of her grasp. I walked home in the darkness alone with the plywood, the saw, and the echo of her cries, which I can hear even now: "Isn't that so? Tell the truth. You'll come."

The following morning I went to Hasqail's store. It was closed, and so was Mukhlif's store. Also Sasoon's, Moshe's, and Haroun's, and all the other Jewish neighbors in the Atami market. I thought nothing of their absence. I didn't ever remember them saying that they would leave Iraq. I didn't relate the closing of the stores to their journey, or Umm Salim's offer to take the furnishings and whatever else until a few days later, when the vacancies in the market attracted other store owners. Then the guessing began. We found out that they had all gone to Palestine, and I would never again see Sami, Sumaya, their mother, or Mukhlif.

The world went dark in my eyes. Sami had had a greater influence on me than any other friend. I ran to the *khan al-bazazeen,* went up the stairs, and stood in the yard where Sami and I had made cars out of wire and read Egyptian magazines.

I could see and hear Sami as he pulled the pistol from his belt and shouted "Hands up!" The bullets resounded in space as they finished off his enemies, cutting the air, leaving their mark on the ether, taking root in the depths, refusing to be forgotten. A tear rolled from my eye. I wiped it away.

Sitting there on the steps as I had so many times with Sami, I recalled the great crime we had committed a few years before. We must have been about seven or eight years old, no more. My father had sent me to the Al-Aghwath Mosque to take some cantaloupe and bread by way of lunch to Abdul-Sami'a, the blind muezzin. Sami had gone with me. He would never go into the mosque except with me. He was afraid of the other children, who knew that he was Jewish. The only time he would go was to use the bathroom, like the rest of us.

There were at least six facilities at the Al-Aghwath mosque. The doors were low, and did not lock from the inside. The etiquette was that you had to knock on the door before opening it. If you heard an "ahem" you didn't open it. I would wait in front of the door till Sami was done. He would often stay and listen to the sounds of the bowel as it emptied its contents, commenting on them, and, because he had seen a lot of war movies, he had gathered a great number of appropriate words. He would comment on each sound that emerged from the bowel: a pistol shot, a cannon shell, a machine gun, artillery. We would stay a while, laugh, and then leave hurriedly.

On that day, however, we had to wait for the muezzin Abdul-Sami'a. Abdul-Sami'a would not allow us to see what was in his room. When we knocked on his door, we head a voice saying, "Yes, just a moment." Most of the time he would ask me to go and wash my hands well and peel the cantaloupe for him. But today he wasn't there. I didn't know what to do. I shouted from behind the door, "Uncle Abdul-Sami'a! I have to go!"

His voice was weak. "Leave them on a paper by the door."

I looked at Sami and said, "Get me a paper from Haroun."

Haroun was the closest of the Jews to the mosque. Sami went to fetch some of the brown paper that was used to wrap goods. He brought back a piece big enough to hold both the melon and the bread if they weren't wrapped. I put it on the floor to the right of the door in the angle between the door and the wall and set the melon and the bread on it. Then I told Abdul-Sami'a where to find it.

The noon prayer had ended a little while before. The mosque was empty except for a few men who were praying under the wide dome. As he looked up at the old minaret, Sami said, "Have you ever been up there?"

"No."

He whispered, "We could go up there and come back down fast. What do you say?"

I looked around, saw no one, and said, "Let's go."

We ran. We were surprised to find that the minaret steps were so small, only about a dozen centimeters wide. We took the steps three or four at a time. The staircase was a spiral, circling around the stone core of the minaret. When we reached the platform at the top, we were overcome with terror. We both stood still, leaning our backs against the stone core; we didn't dare approach the edge of the platform for fear of falling, because it looked as if it were about to collapse. The rays of the sun fell on us, but there was a cool spring breeze. The minaret was old and covered with worn-out plaster. It was no more than thirty meters high and overlooked a large and ugly stretch of the broad, shabby facade of the market that showed the stylistic accretions of the many centuries of history the market had witnessed. It shambled on toward the El-Toub door and the Saraya market, devoid of beauty except for the doves that perched there.

All this was very different from the eastern view, which opened onto virgin nature where the iron bridge slept in eternal wisdom over the green Tigris and the other shore teemed with people, beautiful young women washing skeins of wool by beating them with a wooden bat called a *khatour*. When a young woman struck with the *khatour*, the sound didn't reach us immediately. It arrived a few seconds later, after the *khatour* had been lifted again. The fishing boats were scattered across the wide river, moving in random directions; fishermen's nets flew through the air like magical umbrellas gathering the spirits of the ancient river goddesses, before falling into the water. Thousands of gulls performed their eternal wedding dance above the quiet water, above the swimmers escaping the hot summer.

A large garden overlooked the left bank with its tall green trees, blessed by the sun's rays. "How beautiful the view is!" Sami said.

I answered, "Yes, it's very beautiful."

He looked into my eyes, pleading, and said, "Why don't you call to prayer?"

"Prayer time is over. The noon prayer ended a while ago."

He smiled, quizzically. "Do you know how to call to prayer?"

"Sure."

"Me, too."

I said, "You can't call for prayer!"

"Why?"

"If you say, 'Mohammed is God's prophet,' you become a Muslim and can never go back to being a Jew. You'll be killed if you do. Those are the rules. Have you asked your parents?"

He thought for a while and said, "What if I say half of the call to prayer, and you say the rest?"

"Like this, quietly," I whispered, and he nodded in agreement. "OK, you start."

Sami whispered, *"Allahu akbar, allahu akbar."* Then—and I don't know how—he lost control over his voice, his voice got louder, and with all his might he shouted, "I believe that there is no God but God! *Ashhadu anna la ilah ila allah!"*

I tugged on his dishdasha with all my strength. He almost fell, and I shouted, "What was that? We said we were going to whisper! There are going to be people all over the place! Let's get out of here before anyone hears us. I'm going to leave you here if you don't come right now!"

I started down and he followed. When we reached the ground, one of the men who had been praying walked out, his eyes full of fury. He screamed at us, "What a racket! You little devils, don't you have any morals? You think this is a playhouse?"

He threw his shoe at us and hit me in the leg, I almost fell but kept running. What fear overtook us! We were terrified of being captured. If they had found out Sami was a Jew, they might have killed him. We didn't stop till we arrived in front of our fathers' shops, out of breath. His face was pale like turmeric. He said to me, "They'll kill me. I'm going home. Tell my father that's where I am." He ran off.

When I reached my father's store, the news had already arrived. He asked me, "How could you do that?"

The guilt was killing me. I said, "I just wanted to see the minaret."

"Who was with you?"

"My friend Ghanem," I lied.

I detected a look of doubt in his eyes, but he didn't investigate further. He might have felt some guilt, because he was the one who had sent me to the mosque.

I used to laugh whenever I remembered that incident, but I blamed myself for it. It could have been disastrous if any of those fanatics had found out who it was that had mocked the call to prayer. But it passed; the accomplices are gone. Sami disappeared forever just a couple of years after that incident, and nothing remains but the memory.

I went down the stairs, dispirited, and ran from the market to the Jewish quarter. The narrow alleys were dark, empty, and sad. There were no children playing in the street; no one was there but ghosts. I stood at the house door and knocked but no one answered. I looked through the keyhole and my eyes fell on several bamboo chairs, a wild red rose, and parts of the circular garden wall. I knocked again. A sad, painful echo mingled with the beat of my heart.

The *louzina* peddler was passing by with his tray of sweets, the time-honored delicacy that goes back to the Abassids and was mentioned in the *Arabian Nights*. He stopped when he saw me. Perhaps he noticed the struggle of emotion in my features, or my tearful red eyes. He was in his fifties. He took the wooden crate off of his shoulders and the *louzina* tray off his head, set the tray on the crate and looked at me tenderly, shaking his head. He said in a deep voice, "You're not the only one who misses them. A lot of us do. We've lost them, and they've lost us. But their loss is greater because they've lost their homeland. It's God's will."

His voice quavered and I thought he was going to cry. I could see that—like me—he had had loved ones here. He took out his razor and cut off a piece of *louzina* and handed it to me. "Here. It's free."

I shook my head in refusal and hurried away out of his sight.

I often think, how do we love people? Why we love them, I don't know. Science states that there are chemical compounds in the human body that can coincide with the compounds of another body and thus cause an attraction between the two. I don't find this convincing. I had by chance met three people whose departure tormented my heart. I loved all three, with all my heart and soul. Did some chemical compound cause this love, or was it coincidence? To this day I can't express the feelings I had when Selam, Madeleine, or Sumaya sat near me. I don't know if it was elation, happiness, dissolution, or joy. All the emotions that

I and others have not been able to describe or define, we have called love. Is it the right word? I don't know.

My father passed away in 1956, and my uncle Abdul Hamid took over the store.

In 1963 I was imprisoned for political reasons. My imprisonment lasted a year and a day. The memory of those three beautiful people helped to overcome the misery of prison and helped the time to pass. I thought a lot about writing, but the prison was very crowded. There was no room for privacy anywhere.

I was freed from prison, and in mid-1964 traveled to Morocco to teach at the Ibn Yassin high school in Al Mahmadiye. One day in 1965, while I was teaching my class, Si Saber, the school accountant, sent the janitor, Abu Ali Al-Hajj, with a message asking that I see him during the break. On entering his room he showed me a large brown envelope that had come from Iraq, with several Iraqi stamps, and asked, "Can I have the stamps?"

I laughed and said, "Is that why you sent for me?"

He laughed too, then looked at me seriously and said, "I'm leaving before you today. I'm afraid someone else is going to take them."

I tore open the envelope and handed him the beautiful Iraqi stamps. I was surprised to find another envelope inside, a square pink envelope, unlike the usual rectangular ones, with a Cypriot stamp on it. The stamp was a reproduction of a painting of a sailing ship moving over the waves. I believe it was a painting by a famous European artist, whose name I don't recall. After a little thought, I figured out how this letter from Cyprus must have reached my uncle. It arrived at the Atami market, and when he saw my name he placed it, without opening it, in the large brown envelope, and took it over to my mother after closing the store. They were both illiterate, so they must have taken the envelope to my sister's house at Bab Lakash and had her write my address. My uncle Abdul Hamid was as religious as my father; to him the letter was a trust and it was his duty to send it to its rightful owner. He must have placed the pink letter in the large brown envelope without allowing anyone to read it, and taken it personally to the post office.

Pink is the color of love. I knew no one in Cyprus. I certainly had no lover in Cyprus! Who could this letter be from? I turned the envelope over and didn't find a return address. I opened it and found a postcard with a picture of a very beautiful brown-skinned girl with long black hair parted in the middle that fell into beautiful curls. She had flashing, bewitching eyes. The features were familiar. I turned the picture over and saw the word *Sumaya* written in a wobbly but readable Arabic. Under the signature were blue squares that reminded me of the decorations that I had taught her to make. The decorations were surrounded by a red decorative heart. There was also an address in Cyprus for someone Greek; I could not tell if it was for a man or a woman. I looked at the cancellation—it had been sent eight days earlier. It must have reached Iraq in two days, and as usual it took six days to reach me.

Sumaya! My heart was beating. Was I dreaming? Fourteen years had passed, a lifetime. I thought I was the only sentimental person on earth, but no, someone else had not forgotten. Had anyone but Si Saber been with me they would have heard my heart beating. How did the blood suddenly rush to my face? I touched my cheek, forehead, chin, and mouth, where Sumaya used to plant her warm, unending kisses. I felt weak and I sat down. Si Saber noticed and cried, "Your class has started. What's wrong? Are you sick?"

He approached me and noticed the letter in my hand. "God forbid, is it bad news?"

"No, happy news."

"Why are you dying, then?"

I smiled. "It's happiness. I'm going to Cyprus."

He laughed heartily. "You're not going anywhere."

"How do you know?"

"Didn't you know I can read fortunes?"

Si Saber loved to tease, but he was kind and loving. There were more than seventy-four days till spring break, enough time for a letter to reach her and get back to me. What would I write? I couldn't write a word. Memory overcame me. I spent that evening wasting time with Al Qadiri. I let him do all the talking. I had a strong drink but it didn't quiet my uneasy soul. I drifted off at one in the morning without having written a word.

In the morning my mind wandered while Fatima began to read, in her shy, mellow voice, the Arabic essay she had written. I was anxious to get home and write.

I wrote several pages. I first wrote about Sumaya's mother, whom I loved dearly and who had graciously taken me into her home and been generous with her affection. I wrote about her father and Sami, whom I missed whenever memory took me back to childhood, and about Salim. I told her how I still remembered those beautiful times, how I still felt her kisses burning my cheeks and her arms around my neck. And how I could still taste the *sharab* and honey on her warm tongue. And I still remembered the last words I heard her say: "Stay with us, don't go! You'll come with us. Isn't that so? Tell the truth. You'll come."

I never forgot those words and never will, for as long as I live. I told her that the happiness I felt on receiving her letter was unsurpassed. I wanted to tell her that getting her letter made me even happier than my liberation from prison, but I didn't want to worry her. There would be plenty of time for us to tell each other what had happened in the past few years. I did tell her, however, how I had cried on seeing her father's store closed; how I had gone up to the warehouse with tears in my eyes, gone to their house and seen the closed doors; and how I had looked through the keyhole and seen the red wild rose. I told her about the *louzina* peddler and said she must remember the taste of that delicious treat. I told her about my determination never to lose her again. I asked her to choose anywhere in Europe where we could meet. I said that should we ever meet, nothing would ever separate us but death. When I finished writing I placed the letter on the table. It was about seven in the evening, the time when we would go in search of a friend to pass the time with until bedtime.

There was a knock on the door, and my three friends came in: Si Saber, Al Baqali, and Al Khitabi. They were anxious to hear what I had written. Si Saber said that the grapevine at Ibn Yassin high school had spread the news of what had happened. Al Khitabi could not believe that love like this existed. He said, "This only happens in dreams."

I told him I couldn't believe it either. I was astonished to see the letter in Si Saber's hands. They passed around the picture, remarking on her beauty. Al Khitabi said, "Brother, you are lucky, lucky, lucky."

I agreed as I served them the *sharab*.

Si Saber raised his glass and said, "We're the lucky ones—he came all the way from Iraq to entertain us with these capers." He hesitated, looking at the others, and said, "Don't drink yet—he has to take a vow first."

"What kind of vow?"

"When the answer to your letter arrives, you will not read it alone. You will read it in front of all of us."

The others agreed. I laughed and said, "I agree."

"To Sumaya's health."

"Not even Laila's madman loved so much."

Al Qadiri said, "Here's to the surprise of the twentieth century."

A storm of emotions overwhelmed me after sending the letter. Within two weeks I wrote a beautiful short story. I went with my friends to the shores of the Atlantic, where we sat by the wreck of an old French ship that had gone onto the rocks on a stormy night several years earlier and foundered. We would go there once every couple of weeks to read the poetry that one of us had chosen. There was no one to hear us but the unlucky ship, of which only the bow could be seen, eaten away by the salt and the battering of the waves. The wind, the space, the calm ocean, the ruined ship, and the rocks were no doubt enraptured by the poetry of Al Sayab, Al Bayati, Nazik, Al Muhandis, Ibrahim Naji, Shawqi, Salaah Abdul Sabour, and others. I read the story I had written, which was greatly admired by Al Khitabi, who repeated it over and over again.

My trio of friends and I had decided that three weeks were sufficient for the arrival and return of a letter from Sumaya. Later we added another week, to give her enough time to think of a reply.

Three weeks passed, and then a fourth, a fifth, and a sixth, and nothing happened. Sadness overwhelmed me, and my friends pretended to forget about it. I told them, "She's not going to answer."

"Why?"

"Because she hasn't sent anything since the first letter, only one picture, nothing else. She must have just momentarily recalled an emotion or an incident from the past, as we often do, and once her life was back to normal she forgot all about it."

Si Saber thought a minute and said, "I think you're right. Just a passing memory.

Al Qadiri smiled and said, jokingly, "I think she's married. Maybe she had a fight with her husband, thought about you, and then they made up."

Al Khitabi laughed and said, "She tried to make you her substitute husband."

That was on a Friday. We had spent the evening at Al Khitabi's watching Real Madrid play Manchester United. I wanted the Spanish team to win because I disliked the British for what they had done in Iraq. Al Khitabi disliked the Spaniards for their occupation of Ceuta and Melilla and wanted the British to win. Al Qadiri was from Tetouan but had nothing against the Spaniards; he didn't care who won. He had been involved with a very conservative Spanish girl who gave him only kisses and teased him. His heart was on fire with yearning, and he had decided to marry her in a year after completing the baccalaureate and getting a higher salary. Si Saber disliked all colonizers—British, Spanish, and French. However, he regarded all peoples as his brothers, and enjoyed the art of soccer.

The following day, Saturday, a letter arrived, unexpectedly, in the same wobbly handwriting. Abu Ali Al-Hajj took it from the postman and delivered it personally. Si Saber was late; he didn't come in until ten that morning. It was the same pink envelope, but I didn't open it. I left the classroom and went running to Al Khitabi's room and showed him the letter from a distance. His eyes lit up. Al Qadiri wasn't there that day. I waited for Si Saber to arrive, went to his room, and waved the letter without saying anything. He thought for a moment, then slapped his forehead and said, "I'd forgotten all about it. How stupid I am!"

I said, "Take it, I don't think I can control myself."

I went home alone, had a light lunch, and then took two aspirins that made me sleepy. I awakened around five in the afternoon and walked to a café across from the historic Bab Al-Qasaba, the Casbah. I enjoyed the bitter taste of their black coffee, which reminded me of the thick Iraqi coffee. Just before six, the three friends showed up.

We went home; Si Saber had brought along a bottle of whiskey. We toasted Sumaya, and then love. We didn't read the letter until we were ready for the second toast.

I opened the envelope gently. They were all anxious to hear the contents.

My precious love, I am so happy you went to our house. I miss it so much! Oh, if we had only stayed there. I yearn for one hour in Mosul. What an age has gone by, my love! I am alone. My father passed away, and my mother died a month after she was told that I was supposed to die soon.

I stopped reading. I didn't want to read more bad news. I couldn't believe my eyes. "Did you understand anything?" I asked.

Si Saber said, "Read, things will get clearer."

I went on.

You said in your letter, I will not accept losing you again, for as long as I live. And you asked me to choose a place in Europe were we could meet. You said that should we meet in the future, nothing but death will separate us. How true! I wish my health were normal, so that I could have done what you wanted. But fate is stronger than all of us. I haven't forgotten you for a moment. You have been with me, or I with you, I don't know. I wanted to see you long before now. But I was unable to do so. I dreamed of traveling just to see you. But before I could leave, my doctors informed me that my old sickness, bone cancer, was back—the same disease that Asma had. I am luckier; I have lived longer. My parents knew, but believed in miracles whose time has passed. They hoped my body would overcome the disease. They never crossed me; they spoiled me and never denied me anything I wanted. But fate is stronger than they were. I don't want you to be sad. I beg you to forget me. Don't allow my memory to sadden you or affect the path of your life. Remember me as a child, the child that hugged you, kissed you, and sat in your lap. Don't think of how I have ended up.

I couldn't go on reading. I handed the letter to Al Khitabi, and he read two sentences and then started to cry. Al Qadiri took over, and was able to control himself.

Try to be happy. Get married. You will have a little girl who will look like me. You will see me in her eyes, you will see me in all children's eyes. We were angels. And life to our eyes was more beautiful than paradise. Try to see the world through the eyes of angels. If you have a little girl, and you will, don't deny her anything. Spoil her as my parents did. Children are delicate and can't stand pain.

They inherit the sins of brutal and stupid generations that think of nothing but bygone glory. I wish I could go back in time to live just one hour with you, in our alley, our home, with my innocent girl friends, or just with you. I wish I could play in the yard around the circular garden if only for ten minutes, chasing after each other as we used to do. But my hands are tied. I have no choice. What injustice we lived! They forbade us to live in the place we loved, then forbade us to die there, too! I always asked my parents, "Why didn't you leave me to die there?" Their reply was tears. What a tyrannical equation: They usurped the land we loved, and usurped our right to die in it. My love, don't just look at the past. A thousand kisses. Yours, Sumaya.

PART SEVEN

Ghasoub and Ghadban

Things were moving at a normal pace in our school until the day when the English teacher, Mr. Abdul Alim, exploded the third atom bomb (after Hiroshima and Nagasaki) while teaching Cervantes's *Don Quixote*. Addressing a group of students, one of them being Ghasoub, he posed the question in English, "What was the animal Sancho Panza rode on?" Ghasoub closed his eyes, his face turned shades of red and green, and he didn't utter a sound. At that point Mr. Abdul Alim placed the chalk on the blackboard tray and made a comment that was totally unrelated to Don Quixote and his "emasculated" chivalry, skinny horse, or long lance. It was unrelated to the great genius of Cervantes, or Spain— which, according to our deceased teacher Mr. Shathil Taqa, had been stolen from us. It had no relation to the "colonial English language" that Mr. Abdul Alim was trying to drill into our heads instead of teaching us French—the language of temptation, sexuality, romance, and aesthetics—or Russian, the language of the nation of workers and progressive struggle. However, it was not too distant from the main subject, which linked Sancho Panza's comically obese donkey to all the oppressed animals of the world. Mr. Abdul Alim said, "Nature never sends coincidental messages. There is always a reason for each incident." He let us ponder that for a moment and then went on: "Whenever I am sitting in my room reading and listening to songs by Fairouz, Asmahan, or Abdul Wahab coming from the radio in our house or the neighbor's, I open the window and see either a robin singing in a tree, a cooing dove, or a child laughing. However, when the song I hear is by Farid Al-Atrash, on opening the window I only see a braying donkey. He began to imitate Farid Al-Atrash: "Ha, Ha, Ha, Ha." The imitation was perfect; he could have been Farid Al-Atrash. Then suddenly he began to bray like a donkey.

All the students laughed. That was typical of Mr. Abdul Alim's wonderful and distinctive style, which he used to overcome the monotony of the lessons and the weight of the subject at hand.

With this explanation, Mr. Abdul Alim stirred up a whirlwind that would not die down. Had Ghasoub not been with us, there would not have been any repercussions, and I would have long forgotten the incident.

We were in the fourth year of secondary school. Ghasoub was more than six feet tall, stylish, well built, and well muscled, with a fitting name (derived from the root meaning "force" or "usurpation") because he was strong and appeared to be at least five years older than the rest of us. We never saw him smile and he would never sit with us, but always sat apart in the far right corner of the classroom. He seemed not to see us as he passed us by.

He had, though, befriended another student named Ghadban, who was from the same class but in a different section. Ghadban was also tall, but he was thin and had smiling features, contrary to his name, which meant "angry." Were they related? No one knew. How did they become friends? No one knew. All we knew was that they isolated themselves from the rest of the students, and during recess would walk together along a distant wall. Having read the famous heroic story of Antara Bin Shadad Al-Absi, I knew that Ghasoub and Ghadban were the names of the sons he had by his beloved, beautiful wife Abla.

Ghasoub and Ghadban's facial features were different; they could not have been brothers. Ghasoub had a pale complexion, elongated face, and full lips, while Ghadban had a bronze complexion, narrow eyes, and a broad mouth with thin lips. None of us dared to approach Ghasoub or talk to him. His detachment made us all fear him. Ghadban, however, was friendly and talkative, but we never asked him about his relationship with Ghasoub. Were they relatives or casual friends? We didn't want Ghasoub to know we were interested in knowing more about him, as we didn't want to anger him.

I don't know who came up with the provocative news that these two giants, when they weren't around us, spent their time imitating Farid Al-Atrash. Human nature dictates that when you are in doubt you try to find out for sure, and so we did. More than one of us had seen Ghasoub sing Farid Al-Atrash's songs while swaying his head with the music. Ghadban would first listen, and then join in. What was going on? Iraqis, especially the young men, were divided into two groups: some liked Abdel Wahab, and others liked Farid Al-Atrash. Most of the women liked Umm Kalthoum, while others liked Asmahan and thought that Umm Kalthoum had a hand in her early demise. The arguments and division continued even after Abdul Halim Hafiz and Fairuz started to become popular. Neither Abdul Halim's short, sweet songs, nor Fairuz's radiant songs of modern music and poetry, could change public opinion, or compete with the four original singing giants. Back then, Egyptian songs were heard all over Iraq. The Iraqi government radio network used to play ten Egyptian songs to one Iraqi song. Thursday nights, however, remained without competition, devoted to Umm Kalthoum.

It was in this furiously competitive atmosphere that Mr. Abdul Alim exploded his atom bomb at school. His statement seemed to have the weight of logic and authority; he often let himself digress in brilliant discourses; and few classes ended without our vision having been broadened in a highly enjoyable fashion.

Every bomb sets off an equal and opposite reaction. I don't know when the storm began or who started it.

None of us knew whether Mr. Abdul Alim had known of Ghasoub's love for Farid Al-Atrash. Knowing would have required investigative abilities that were beyond him. How then was he led from Ghasoub's lack of response to the question he had asked him to his mockery of Farid Al-Atrash and the donkey? No one could answer this question. It could have been a coincidence. Only God knows what is hidden from our eyes.

The first reaction occurred a few days later. Before class one of the students walked in singing a Farid Al-Atrash song that was echoed by another student who made braying sounds. Then things took a turn for the worse as two other students joined in, one participating in the song and the other braying. Those who—like me—had no such talents merely laughed.

I imagine that Ghasoub and Ghadban could no longer take it, and after a week they stopped coming to school. When eventually they returned, they were met with an enormous tumult made up of innumerable students, half singing Farid Al-Atrash songs, and the other half making braying sounds. Most of the secondary school students participated in this event; the noise reached the principal's office and teachers' lounge. One of the students swore that the effect was so strong that the doves that usually perched on the northern school wall were singing Farid Al-Atrash songs, while the crows brayed like donkeys. Matters did not stop there: students took to gathering in the playground during recess and displaying their new-found talents. The issue became worrisome and demanded action, and so the principal intervened. He was an eloquent speaker with a powerful personality that demanded respect. He gathered all the students in the school-yard. Each class gathered in front of its classroom and he began to chastise us: "What is all this? Do you like the braying of donkeys? Go to the forest or villages where you'll be able to see thousands of donkeys and turn into to donkeys and jackasses yourselves. Bray all you want there. And if you like being donkeys, stay there and don't come back to Mosul, which has enough donkeys. There's no place for donkeys in this school. This is a respected school, not a farm for donkeys and jackasses and other livestock. I forbid the sound of braying. This behavior is immoral. You are behaving like elementary students. Don't force me to treat you like hoodlums and underachievers. From this moment on, I will assign a teacher to roam the playground at recess and report any student who transforms himself to a donkey. He who does so will be immediately sent to join the animals."

Mr. Abdul Fatah, the elegant Arabic language teacher whose hair was always carefully combed with Brylcreem, was assigned to the playground watch. We saw him walking the playground during the following recess, holding a yellow bamboo whip that could give your hand a nasty burn. The day passed without singing or braying. The following day, however, another tactic was put into place whereby songs were hummed and then accompanied by hummed braying.

Ghasoub and Ghadban stayed away from school again. The singing exchanges stopped. However, the incidents were constantly recalled, and then one day Mr. Abdul Alim did not show up for the first or the second period. He was in fact absent the whole day. We found out from his colleague that he had been at the hospital overnight, due to a broken arm and a broken nose caused by a fall on the street. And so a group of the smartest students of English, the "language of the filthy colonialists," including Bilal Al-Hirthi, Hilal Abdel-Masih, Abdel-Qader Omar, and others went to visit him in the hospital. He was in a sad situation. His head was wrapped with gauze, and his arm was plastered and placed in a sling over his head. He had had an operation for the readjustment of his nose. He was, fortunately, able to converse in spite of the gauze wrap. He told them that he would return to school in a week, though his arm would still be in a sling. A broken arm takes forty-five days to heal. But thankfully the break was in the left and not the right arm.

He had slipped and fallen. It was no one's fault; it had been an act of God. But we suspected that Ghasoub and Ghadban had had something to do with the accident, and we began to fear them more, especially when they both returned to school on the day that Mr. Abdul Alim was first absent. Ghasoub had also changed his tactic; he would walk among us and look at us with mean and threatening eyes. He could have knocked out any of us with one blow. All comical and sarcastic actions, all the artful imitation of Farid Al-Atrash, stopped. The sounds of braying donkeys ceased. No one dared imitate either. The question, however, remained: did they have a hand in the accident?

Time passed, and we each went our way. One day in 1979 I was amazed to see Ghasoub before me on the Golden Sands Beach in Zalatny on the Black Sea near Varna, Bulgaria. I was seated with my wife and two children in the Golden Fish Restaurant, which served fresh fish and had a wonderful view of the sea. I saw Ghasoub's giant frame coming out of the sea. He had put on some weight and had a small belly, but was still as fit as ever. It seemed that he had been swimming in the Black Sea with his wife and two young men, about sixteen and eighteen, and a young girl about fourteen years old. His wife was very beautiful and fit like him; she even resembled him a bit. I was immediately taken back to the chaos that had started with Fairuz, Farid Al-Atrash, and the robins and the donkeys, and which had ended with Mr. Abdul Alim in the hospital. I had the urge talk to him, but I didn't, though he sat at a table not far from me.

Three days later, the ideal situation for meeting Ghasoub again came up in Varna. My wife and children went to sleep around nine, but I was in the habit of going to bed no earlier than eleven. I took my book and went to a nearby hotel café that had no tourists. As I entered the café I saw Ghasoub drinking a bottle of beer. I walked toward him, greeted him, and with his permission took a seat at his table. "Ghasoub, how are you?"

He glared at me and asked, "Do you know me?"

"Yes, we were schoolmates."

"Where?"

"In the fourth secondary at the Eastern Secondary School."

He smiled and said, "That was a long time ago."

"Yes."

He laughed uncertainly, as if he could not believe that someone could know him, and said, "So you know me?"

"Yes."

We both sipped on our drinks. I said, "If you don't mind, I'd like to ask you a question."

"Please."

"Do you like Farid Al-Atrash?"

He stared into my eyes and must have recalled those days. He thought a little and then said, "Why do you ask?"

I didn't hesitate: "You must have been very upset by those boyish pranks."

"Yes, very much."

I repeated the question about Farid Al-Atrash. He smiled and said, "He's love itself."

He fell silent. I thought he didn't want to talk, but he started laughing. He looked at me and said, "I loved my cousin, but I was forbidden to see her. They wouldn't let me in their house unless her father or brothers were there; and whenever the men sat together they would forbid all the women to sit with us except for my uncle's wife. They were very strict."

"What did loving your cousin have to do with Farid?"

"I knew she loved me, and she would purposely sing a Farid Al-Atrash song while I visited with my uncle and male cousins. I would hear her sing, and begin to wilt in my seat."

"Didn't they object to her singing, since they were that strict?"

"They didn't know that she knew I was there."

I was moved by the thought of his long ordeal, loving a cousin he was forbidden to see. "How long did that last?"

"Six years. They tried to marry her off many times, but she refused. They would not allow me to see her until I graduated from college and went with my whole family—my father, mother, and brothers—to ask for her hand."

I remembered Abdul Wahab and his suffering, but Ghasoub's seemed to have been fiercer yet.

"How did you fall in love with her, if you never saw her?"

"I've loved her since we were young."

In his eyes I could see a unique love story, one to test the heart of a giant whose soul nobody would expect to be capable of such devotion and tenderness.

"Is she the one that was with you at the Golden Fish Restaurant?"

His eyes lit up. "Were you spying on me?"

I laughed. "No. I was at the restaurant and saw all of you coming out of the water. I remembered."

He laughed and said, "I know what you mean."

"The story of Mr. Abdul Alim."

He laughed. "You remember that."

"How can I forget? Did you have a hand in it?"

He nodded. "Yes."

"How is it that he didn't identify and accuse you?"

"He couldn't."

"Why?"

"He never saw me."

I smiled and wondered how they could have been missed. They were both giants. "You were both too big to disappear."

He laughed heartily. "King sized!"

I smiled. "Exactly."

"We knew when he returned home in the evening, and so we used rocks to break the one light that lit the street. It was dark."

"You pushed him?"

"No. If we'd pushed him, he would have felt it and reported it to the police."

"What did you do?"

"We tripped him. He always walked very fast, almost running. We each held on to one end of a rope, and he tripped over it. The fall was bad because we had put a rock next to the rope intending for him to fall on his face, and that's what happened. We thought he was dead. He moaned for a couple of minutes and then fell silent, and we sneaked away."

He looked into the distance and said, "That was our only choice. We had to choose between bringing him down and our future. If we hadn't done that, we wouldn't have been able to go back to school. When I heard later that he had returned to the country and was assigned to the university, I went to him and confessed. I apologized, quite profusely, and he was very gracious about it, though he had forgotten the whole incident."

PART EIGHT

Hajim and Sabika
and a Long Night of Love

"Look what he's done to me!" Sabika said it as she lifted her worn-out dress up to her navel, and for the first time in my life I saw a woman's pubic area, where the thick black hair lay matted at the confluence of her brown thighs. My eyes fixed on two dark smears of blood congealed on her upper thighs, and a long line of blood, also black, running down the right thigh.

Sabika did not usually knock on our door in daytime. She simply pushed the door open and walked in as any member of our family would. I had a bad cold that day that had kept me from going to the market, and I had been sleeping at the front of the large room, next to the noisily spinning Japanese KDK fan that cooled the brutally hot Mosul summer air.

Sabika was almost my mother's age, and was ninety-nine percent blind. Her pupils were nearly all covered by the cloudy whitish-yellow irises. She only saw shadows, and could not make out who was in front of her. She recognized people by their voices and was unable to tell who they were unless they spoke. Children would often tease her by standing in her way, causing her to bump into them. She would laugh her pleasant laugh and begin the guessing game: "God bless you, who are you?"

Whenever I asked my mother why Sabika had no family, she would reply by looking up toward heaven and saying, "It's God's will."

My mother screamed at the sight of the blood splotches on Sabika's thighs. "Oh, you poor *msakhameh!*" This was a word meaning "soot-blackened" which was also used for raped or violated women. "Who did this to you?"

Sabika let her dress down and came and sat next to my mother on the wet, cooled mat.

"Who else but him?"

"When did he come?"

"Last night."

"Why all this blood?"

Sabika began to cry. "If you only knew."

"What?"

She didn't answer, but went on crying.

"Is it painful?"

"Yes."

"Come with me. Get up. I'm taking you to the clinic."

Sabika begged her: "Shield me, and may God shield you. They'll see my private parts. I don't want to be the talk of the town. What will they think?"

"All right, come and let me clean your wounds."

"With what?"

"We have alcohol. The clinic gave some to Mustafa a month ago when a nail pierced his foot."

Mother placed a pillow on the mat and gently helped Sabika lie down on her back. She lifted Sabika's dress up to her navel, and I was able to see everything clearly. Being blind, Sabika didn't know I was in the room. Had she known, she would have refused to uncover even an inch of her body. I remained silent. My mother must have thought the fever had knocked me out, or she wouldn't have let Sabika uncover herself in front of me. Mother cleaned the wounds on Sabika's thighs with cotton soaked in alcohol as Sabika moaned and groaned from the pain. To calm her down my mother questioned her. "Did he come in the morning, like the garbage man?"

"No, he came in the evening, and he wasn't alone. I think there were four other men."

"Where did they sleep?"

"In the ruins."

"Did you have enough mattresses?"

"They used what I could gather for pillows, and slept on their cloaks."

Once my mother was done, she helped Sabika straighten up. Sabika covered her thighs and said to my mother, "I want to ask you something."

"What is it?

Sabika began to cry again. My mother said, "Are your wounds hurting you? Don't worry, the pain will go away in a few minutes."

Sabika choked on her tears and said, "No, it isn't the wounds."

"What, then?"

"Tell me, is a husband capable of doing it more than ten times a night?"

Neither my mother nor I understood what she meant. My mother asked, "Do what?"

"He did it to me more than ten times."

My mother cried out in distress, "Are you sure?"

"Yes."

"May God strike him! There is no power mightier than God's."

Sabika murmured, "How can you say that?"

Mother didn't reply, but asked in a sharp tone, "Did you tell anyone?"

"No."

After a moment my mother asked again, "Are you sure he did it more than ten times?"

"Maybe more, I'm not sure. As soon as he was done he would roll over and go to sleep, like he always does, and come back just as I started to doze off. He would climb onto me, and if I spoke to him he just grunted. His weight was different each time; sometimes he was light, and sometimes heavy. Even his smell was different each time. I didn't get to sleep till dawn. As soon as I would begin to sleep, he would be all over me again."

I saw my mother wipe tears with the palm of her hand. Then she looked up toward the ceiling and said, "God, why this agony?" It sounded like her words were directed at God, but then she added, "What do you expect from a liar? When he got engaged to you he said he would come to see you once or twice a month. He has never come more than once a year, or every other year, and has never stayed more than two or three days. He deceived us all."

"He's busy."

"Don't deceive yourself by protecting him. Busy? No, you should say he's a liar. Did he give you anything?"

"Yes, he gave me one dinar and told me to give it to Hajim."

It was a very hot day. The black fan spun ineffectually. The day before, I had been at the Tigris, soaking the woven palm baskets. I couldn't figure out why they seemed to weigh more than usual and were harder to pull out of the water. This was just after the Eid, and I was still living in the bitterness of separation from Selam. I paused for a moment and saw a porter leaving the riverbank after soaking his body in the cool water. I asked him to help me put the baskets on my head, and he did so. I felt relief as the cold water dripped onto my hair and body, soaking my dishdasha, and as I walked home, the air chilled me.

I finished the errands assigned to me by my father and the Mad Dog, but that morning I had awakened with a fever and a severe cold, and couldn't get out of bed. And so my mother wouldn't let me go to the market, and Sabika, not knowing I was home, had uncovered herself and told my mother her story.

Sabika was very poor. The only people I knew then that were poorer were Selam and her mother. But Sabika was strongly built and washed people's clothes for a living. Because of her blindness she would often wash the clothes twice to guarantee their cleanliness. Most of the people in our neighborhood were poor, and so Sabika didn't work regularly. She found customers only on occasions such as births, weddings, and deaths. She never stated how much money she wanted for her services; she trusted in her customers' honesty and would say "Thank God" whenever she got paid and would never ask for more. My mother would sometimes talk to her about her right to ask for more, and Sabika's response was always, "Shame on me."

Once she worked for three days in a house, and the housewife gave her fifty fils. Sabika refused to ask for more despite my mother's revolutionary incitement. In Marxian terms, however, she did take one step forward by refusing a couple of months later to work for that woman. The woman realized her mistake and increased Sabika's pay.

Sabika would often work only one day a week. She saved whatever money she made for the son she rarely saw, and refused to spend that money even to satisfy her own hunger. She spent the rest of the days sleeping at Umm Mohammad's. Umm

Mohammad was a widow who had children and lived in a three-room hut. The large room of the hut had a thirty-year-old partially collapsed roof. The two other rooms, however, were intact. Umm Mohammad had arranged the fallen stones into a two-meter high wall that separated the intact rooms where she lived with her children from the room with the collapsed roof where Sabika lived for free. Sabika's area was isolated, and her visitors could neither see nor hear Umm Mohammad or her children.

Sabika had built her "nest" at the front of the collapsed room, where the rain couldn't reach. Ever since I could remember, one of my daily chores had been to take a tray of food to Sabika every evening. My mother would always fix Sabika's tray before serving us. That food was perhaps Sabika's only daily meal. No one in our neighborhood could help her besides us.

Sabika was always stretched out on her so-called mattress when I pushed open the heavy wooden door—which was much like the door that Selam and her mother used to have—and walked toward her with the tray. She would straighten up, smile, and begin panting like a person in search of water in the desert. Long before I reached her, her hands would be stretched out to me, and her voice would rise anxiously. She would be famished, and would say, "Is that you? God bless and give you prosperity." She would take the tray and go on repeating the invocation till I disappeared.

Every year I delivered to her a bundle containing a *thoub* made from chintz that my father would buy and have Mary sew for her, a couple of woolen socks from my father's store, and a pair of slippers that Abi Adnan Al-Imanji, who had the neighboring store, would donate. My mother would add other things to the bundle that we were not allowed to see. I would walk to Sabika's with the bundle under my arm and the tray in my hands. When I got older, my younger brother was asked once to deliver her meal, but instead of taking the tray to Sabika he stood at Umm Mohammad's door, ate the food, left the empty tray behind the door, and ran away to play. He didn't think anyone could see him. The next day, when I was sitting before dark in my usual place on the staircase doing my homework, Sabika brought back the tray as she usually did. She didn't see me, and so she said to my mother, "Why didn't you let Saleh eat before he brought the dinner tray?"

Suspiciously, my mother asked, "Why do you say that?" She wasn't used to long-established habits being questioned.

"Let him eat before he brings my dinner."

My mother was at a loss. "How can we eat before you? There might be nothing left, only leftovers! Are we humans or animals? We're Arabs!"

Sabika withdrew in tears. My mother dropped her washing and ran after her. She hugged her, said she was sorry and whispered, "Does that mean you've had nothing to eat since yesterday?"

Sabika managed to stop crying and said, "Praise be to God."

My mother cried, "God help us!" and ran to the pantry to get the one egg we always kept for emergencies. Lunch had never been an important meal for us; we ate whatever was there: bread and molasses, pickles, bread with oil and sugar, or flat bread boiled in molasses. I knew that my parents wouldn't hold a young child like my brother to his chores, so I told my mother I would continue to deliver Sabika's dinner tray.

"Let me disinfect your wounds again," my mother said. "They have to be disinfected three times to heal fast." I don't know where my mother had learned that, but she was convinced of it. Sabika stretched out again, and my mother went back to work with the alcohol and the cotton.

"Ah!" Sabika wailed in pain, and my mother tried to calm her. "Don't scream. I don't want the neighbors to hear."

I knew that Sabika's wounds were more than she could bear, or she wouldn't have screamed. But I only realized many years later what her husband had done to her. Finally it occurred to me to wonder: was Hajim the son of Imara, Sabika's husband, or of one of the men her husband had brought to lie with her, exploiting her blindness? No one will ever know. Even Jalal Alqibtan, my mother's lawyer cousin, could not answer this vital question. Jalal had been the only one who had seen Imara, twenty years earlier. We had never met him. Not even Sabika, who had agreed to marry him as a result of my mother's insistence, could judge.

Once in a while, I used to see her son Hajim, who was six years older than me. Back then he didn't work; he simply spent the time wasting his mother's money. He had been studying in a religious boarding school and had passed, as I later learned, by cheating, as did all of his colleagues. He graduated from the religious school with little knowledge of the principles of the Arabic language and was accordingly qualified to be a teacher of religion and Arabic. He excelled, however, in lying and hypocritically riding on the shoulders of others; this later attained him a position at the Ministry of Education.

Hajim had never met his father, and had failed in his attempts to meet him after he had become a teacher. Imara had told his wife when he married her that he was from Samawat. Hajim went to Samawat after graduation, and searched the city and its neighboring towns, but was unable to find a trace of his father or his supposed tribe.

Imara had first seen Sabika in the early twenties. When he saw her he followed her to Umm Mohammad's hut and knocked on the door. Umm Mohammad asked what he needed, and he

replied he was there to ask for the dark-complexioned woman's hand in marriage. Umm Mohammad began to cheer; but
Sabika said she needed more time and asked him to come back
the following day; then she came to confer with my mother. All
I remember is that my mother would often tease her: "He fell
in love with you, Sabika." Sabika's bronzed face would turn red
with embarrassment.

When Sabika discovered his name was Zabbala, which means
garbage man, she rejected him for social and humane reasons.
She thought about the feelings of the son she would have in the
future, and how his friends would tease him for being the son of
Al Zabbala. No, that was not acceptable to her.

My mother thought for a while and said: "I will go this
evening to get advice from my lawyer cousin, Jalal. Come back
tomorrow."

The lawyer asked that the man be taken to the courthouse
the following day, if he agreed, to have his name changed to
Imara. When he and Sabika went to the courthouse the next day,
the lawyer asked him if he had a birth certificate or a passport,
and Zabbala replied, "No."

The lawyer then said, "Now listen. Here they're going to
change "Zabbala" to "Imara." Do you agree?"

Zabbala laughed, pointed to his chest and said, "My name
will be registered as Imara? I am Imara? Yes, I accept the name,
Imara is my name."

Jalal smiled and said, "I'll go with you to see the judge and
tell him that your name is Imara. You must answer to that name
from now on."

"Agreed."

The marriage certificate, which was kept by Sabika, was
issued with the husband's name as Imara Bin Sayid Alawi.

I suddenly had a sneezing attack that electrified Sabika. She screamed, "Who's there? Is it your husband? Oh my God, he heard everything!"

My mother reassured her. "Don't worry, it's not my husband, it's only Mustafa. He's sick; he has a high fever and has been asleep."

She calmed down and sighed, "Thank God."

My mother said, "If he comes again, don't let any of his friends come in. Do you understand?"

"I understand, I won't let them in."

My mother repeated her warning. "Don't give in to him."

"No." She nodded her head in agreement.

It was perhaps three months later when I heard her tell my mother that Imara had come with four people and that she had refused to let them in. He got mad and began to shout, but to no avail. At that point he told her she had to either let them all in or he would go away, never to return. She told him, "Do as you please." He left and never came back.

PART NINE

Shafaq

My sister Shafaq lived with us until she was sixteen. Any number of engineers, physicians, and army officers sought her in marriage, but my father preferred that she marry someone who was religious and pious. He chose Qanet for her despite the railing criticism of our relatives for turning down so many distinguished and well-off young men. My father's solemn gaze was enough to deter any objection to his decision. It was a settled matter: Shafaq would marry Qanet. There was no room for discussion.

Qanet was older than Shafaq by four years. He held a poorly paid clerk's position, as he had only an elementary education. Despite his modest wage and his low-status job, he was intelligent and ambitious and he exuded joy and vitality. He was always smiling and laughing. He worked during the day as a mail clerk at the Directorate of Religious Endowments in Mosul and studied at night. When he proposed to Shafaq, he was still in the third intermediate grade and was preparing to sit for official exams. He was expected to pass these exams with distinction, which would allow his father, an influential clergyman, to find him a job with a better salary. He also had plans to go to college. However, his meager salary, along with his refusal to accept financial help from his parents, made it difficult for him to find an appropriate place to live after the marriage. The newly wedded couple had to spend a few days at the groom's parents.

I can't express the profound feelings of emptiness that I felt when I saw the house without Shafaq! Beneath the dull yellow ceiling light in our room, my mother sat in the corner with her head between her knees, and my sisters wept.

Our house was small. The courtyard was small, our room was small, and our cellar was small. I ran down to the cellar, I went up to the rooftop. I ran around the courtyard. I didn't see Shafaq. Where had she gone? I knew she was getting married that same day. However, like any child, I didn't expect my sister to disappear altogether. I was nine or ten years old. I didn't grasp the idea of marriage, separation from family, and the girl's devotion to a new, independent life. I didn't comprehend any of this. Everything in the house—the walls, the pots, the carpet, the courtyard—was whispering "Shafaq." Everything in the house had Shafaq's fingerprints on it.

On my first day of school, Shafaq had helped me put my shoes on right, as I had put them on reversed, and she laced them up for me properly. Shafaq helped me put on my first suit. The first Abu Nuwas joke I read made Shafaq laugh. Shafaq cried—and made the rest of us cry—watching the first Mariam Fakhreddine movie that played in Mosul. Shafaq mended our torn clothes. Shafaq was the one who embroidered our sheets and pillowcases—she filled them with bright flowers so that it felt like springtime all year round.

Shafaq, Shafaq, Shafaq. We had no life without her.

How could Shafaq disappear from our house?

None of us could sleep. Most of the family used to spend the night in the main room, except for me and my little brother, who slept in the small room. However, that night we went down from our room and slept with the rest of them. We lay there listening to each other's weeping. My father had to sit up and recite the Koran in a low voice until we fell asleep. But we woke up in the morning to a gloomy house—lifeless in the absence of Shafaq. We loved her greatly. She was the mainspring of the house: its beautiful face, its wise overseer, and the one who had the last word in it.

Afterward, Shafaq moved into a small house overlooking the Tigris. But she couldn't live there for more than two weeks. The house sat atop a steep drop-off above the river, exposed to strong winds that howled at night, scaring Shafaq and keeping her awake.

She and Qanet moved in with us and occupied the small room where my brother and I used to sleep. Eventually, they found a small house in our neighborhood and settled in. That turned out to be a reasonable solution. Shafaq would spend most of her time with us. Our attention turned to Shafaq's new married life, and we devoted ourselves to her happiness, just as she had devoted herself to us before her marriage.

Shafaq was married when she was sixteen years old. A year later, Shu'a was born. Shu'a was truly, in our eyes, the most beautiful baby boy in the world.

In Shafaq's life there was a small thing that I was proud of: I was twice the cause of her being greatly moved, once to sorrow and once to joy. I introduced her to a world that she would never have entered without me. As a result of my influence in her short life, she used to laugh from the bottom of her heart remembering those two events.

Shafaq was as beautiful as her name, which means "twilight"—the red of the sunset mixed with the brilliance of heaven. She was pale and slender, with black eyes like Selam's, flowing with energy, full of life and love like Sumaya, kind, uncomplicated, and smart. She stood out among my sisters with a unique kind of beauty that comes along only once in a lifetime.

Now, half a century after her death, enough time has gone by for me to patch together an image from deeply rooted memories. Now Shafaq stands out as a paragon, rich in unique traits that no one else can compete with.

Shortly after her marriage, I was able to convince her religiously conservative husband that he and his wife should accompany me to the Summer Crescent Movie Theatre in the Al-Dowasah quarter to watch a film called *The Foundling*. No one expected her husband to agree, not even me. When I think about it now, it makes sense, as he was trying to get me to join the Muslim Brotherhood. Previously, he had given me a book written by Muhammad Qutb and asked me to summarize it. I read a few pages, and then I put it aside to read later. When Mariam Fakhreddine's *The Foundling* was shown, I worked up the courage to make this impossible request of him. I was surprised by his assent. He might have considered it a quid pro quo.

I had read *The Foundling*, by Mohammed Abdel Halim Abdullah, in the Egyptian "Story Club" book series before it became a movie. Whether it was the golden or the silver book, I can't remember. In my opinion at the time, the story was excellent. It gained great fame after it won the Qoot Alquloob "Food for the Heart" prize. The story was a love tragedy. The star was Mariam Fakhreddine, a beautiful actress with "soft angelic features," as she was described by the magazines *Akhar Sa'a* and *Al Musawwir*.

Shafaq was excited by the idea of going to the movie theatre; she had never gone before. Her husband Qanet was supposed to join us at the movie theatre, but he didn't.

I went with her and with my two younger sisters. Mariam Fakhreddine had the role of a beautiful young lady. But she was a foundling. She grew up in an orphanage, well-mannered and good natured, and then she became a nurse devoted to her work and gained the respect and approval of all. As chance would have it, a respected physician from an old prestigious family fell in love with her. As usual, the family rejected the idea of marriage because of her unknown origin. The story ends with the tragedy of the young lady's death.

During the show, most of the audience was crying over the beautiful young woman's wretched luck and her tragic end. My sister Shafaq, however, did not stop crying at the movie theatre like everyone else; instead, she went on crying all the way home. When her husband came in and found her crying, he tried in vain to make her forget about it, but he got nowhere. She went to lie down without eating, and without making dinner for him. She slept lightly only to wake up, remember the story, and start crying again. In the morning she resumed crying. She didn't do anything else. After he gave up on her resuming a normal life, he brought her to our house and said to her in a furious state: "This is your parents' house. Do your crying here, and don't come back until you stop."

Qanet left, very angry. My mother's attempts to get Shafaq to stop crying did not succeed. She would stop for a time, but as soon as she put a bite in her mouth, she would remember what had happened to Mariam Fakhreddine and start crying again. Shafaq's nature was very strange; I don't know who named her

Shafaq. We used to call her "Shafaqa"—which means compassion or pity—instead of Shafaq.

She mastered any job she undertook and she was extraordinarily tidy, but her tender-heartedness trumped everything. Once, when Shafaq was still with us before her marriage, my mother found a mouse in a corner, and asked Shafaq to hand her a stick with which to kill the mouse. Not only did Shafaq refuse to help her kill the mouse, but also she called me and my older sister and told us to look at the beauty of God's creation. Truly, this tiny mouse, less than six centimeters long, was very beautiful. I still remember how extraordinary was the harmony of its form and size, its ears and tail, and its colors: its mouth was dark red, its eyes shiny black, and its hair a pleasing gray. The mouse did not move when it saw us looming over it. It looked at us with an innocent and interested look, as if it were the human and we were the animals from a strange circus. If it had tried to escape it would have succeeded. But it did not even try. It made no effort to move. Maybe it was sick. Shafaq held it in a piece of cloth, making sure not to hurt it while she admired its beauty. She intended to throw it in the street, but my other sister objected, because it would be exposed to stray cats in the neighborhood. There were many of them at that time: a cat would have eaten it within a minute. She sighed in sorrow; if I had known of a safe place I would have thrown it there. Then she raised her eyes to heaven: "My God, why did you create such a beautiful animal to be killed?"

My mother snapped at her in anger, "Beg your Lord for forgiveness! There's no objecting to what God has created."

Shafaq quailed and her eyes were full of tears. I don't know how it occurred to her to ask me to throw the mouse in a cemetery that was nearby in Thalmy, across the street from my school, about two hundred meters away. I obeyed her immediately. I ran with the mouse lying quiet in my right hand. Its beautiful black eyes were looking at me placidly. I didn't know if a tiny animal such as this mouse could think or not. And if it was thinking, did it see itself as it watched people, houses, and places passing by so fast, and did it feel the joy we feel when we are riding in a fast train or a car? I set it down gently at the entrance of the vast fenced cemetery, and came back running to wash my hands under Shafaq's supervision.

When Shafaq got married, I hoped with all my heart that her house wouldn't have any mice in it.

It happened that the Mad Dog came to visit us. His visits were rare, maybe once every three months. He came when he closed his store, choosing the time of his visit carefully, staying for a few minutes and then leaving hurriedly before my father returned from the evening prayers. He was terrified that my father would ban him for his greedy behavior, ill-tempered brutishness, absence from prayers, and addiction to gambling.

When the Mad Dog saw Shafaq crying and found out that I was the one behind the idea, and that I was the one who had taken my three sisters to the movie, he lashed out with a hard punch to my nose and mouth, followed by another one to my forehead, stunning us all. Blood flowed from my nose and mouth. He screamed, "It's all because of you, idiot! What's next, taking your *mother* to the movies?"

We all knew he didn't like Shafaq, or, for that matter, any of us. When Shafaq got married, my mother begged him to put on a banquet for her husband's family to gain face in front of her in-laws. He refused with sarcastic, hurtful words: "Sure, why not? I own a bank, right? I'm here to help everybody and his brother."

This was always his style; he would behave with awful brutality to satisfy his sick character and take revenge on others. My mother rushed to protect me, screaming, "Stop it! You're just looking for an excuse!"

My mother and Shafaq stood between us. If she hadn't intervened, he would have torn me apart. He was taller and stronger than I. Before he left he said in a threatening tone, "I'll go to the library and withdraw your security deposit, to make you stop reading that silly stuff."

I didn't care about the punch, the pain, the flowing blood, my loose tooth, or being able to eat; instead, I was terrified that such an evil idea would come into his rotten head. I can still see his finger pointed at me while he threw that last bomb before slamming the door behind him: "You'll see!"

That would mean a real disaster for me. Managing to save enough money for the library security deposit had been a great accomplishment; it had meant long days of effort, deprivation, and saving. After Miss Khadija discovered my ability to read on the first day of the first grade, she brought me the second-grade reading book. I returned it to her the next day, after reading it in one night. Before the end of the first week, I had read all the books for the elementary level. Then Miss Khadija brought me the reading material for the middle school. I read only the stories and returned the book the next day. After that she asked me if I knew where the public library in Mosul was.

The public library was located on the bank of the Tigris in a splendid, breathtaking building, close to my father's store. If you could put one dinar down as security, they would give you three books to take home to read and return in two weeks. If you didn't have the money, you could read the books you wanted inside the library. I considered going to the library during spring break, but I couldn't work up the courage, as I expected that they would not allow a barefoot child in a dishdasha to enter it. I used to go to the market barefoot so I could run fast on errands for my father and the Mad Dog; if I didn't, I took a smack on the head.

I kept on dreaming and thinking about collecting a whole dinar for the deposit. To have so much money at that time seemed impossible, as my daily allowance was only five to ten fils (equivalent to a penny), and collecting 1000 fils meant that I would deprive myself for more than a hundred days. The only thing left for me was the Eid, the Islamic feast. During the Eid we got more than twice as much as we got on an ordinary day. The only problem with the Eid was that I couldn't control myself. I spent whatever was in my hand that day. I bought the things that I was deprived of on ordinary days. My friend Adnan suggested a fair solution: Buy a clay piggy bank with ten fils, then just put half of your daily allowance in it.

This was genius. I was delighted. He said, "Putting in ten fils every other day is better than depriving yourself for such a long time." I did what Adnan suggested immediately, but the piggy bank stayed light for months. It became like the cat of the familiar story: Though the cat ate a kilogram of meat three times a day, her weight stayed at one kilogram and never increased. After some time, I caught my younger brother in the act of extracting money from the piggy bank with a match stick. When he saw me, he threw it down and ran away. I realized that I would not be able to collect that amount of money even in ten years if the piggy bank was kept in the house and my brother stole from it every day. So I thought I would keep the piggy bank at my father's store, but then I discarded this idea because my brother could distract my father and steal from it while he wasn't paying attention.

I decided that I would stash it with Mukhlif the Jew. Many times, Sami and I used to play in his big store, and I used to nap at his place on summer days. He had a great desire to explore the world. He often asked me to read to him from the magazines that Hamu used to borrow from the merchants in the market. We preferred to read them at his store, especially in winter because we couldn't sit on the cold marble second-floor stairs. Mukhlif always welcomed us. Sometimes there would be five or more of us, as Mahdi, the owner of the landing, or Rasheed Bin Al Safi joined us.

Mukhlif spoke broken Arabic, but he understood everything. He even understood the news bulletins on the radio, even though right up until he disappeared he kept mixing up the male and female forms of address. By way of compensation, he spoke Hebrew, Turkmen, Kurdish, and a little Aramaic. When I handed the piggy bank to him he asked me whether I wanted to buy a dress or a pair of shoes; I told him that I was saving up for a public library security deposit. He didn't understand. I tried in vain several times to explain, but it was useless until Sami came by and explained it to him in Hebrew. Mukhlif patted me on the shoulder in great admiration, pursed his lips, and nodded at me in respect.

There were days when I was terrified of being late for the Mad Dog, so I didn't have enough time to put the money in the piggy bank; those days I used to throw the money in front of Mukhlif and run quickly to finish the errands I was charged with. On school days, I mostly forgot about the piggy bank even when I sat in my father's store while he went to pray.

Then suddenly one day my unemployed bachelor uncle Abdel Hamid showed up. It seems that he had gotten fed up with sitting in the coffee shop from morning until evening, especially when he wasn't able to listen to his beloved singer on the radio. She was his favorite of all the singers, male or female: Zakia George. (Voices of Egyptian, Syrian, and Lebanese singers got the lion's share of exposure on Iraqi radio programs.) My uncle took on the responsibility of helping my father at the store, which released me from going there while he was at noon prayers on school days.

My ceasing to go to the Atami market every day affected my savings plan. When the third grade results were announced, I went to the store the next day to help my father and the Mad Dog for the official start of summer vacation. I had just started listening to Sami's account of a movie he had seen the day before, when I heard Mukhlif calling me. Sami and I went to him, and he asked me, "Did you pass?"

"The results aren't out yet. Maybe in a couple of days."

Sami burst out excitedly, "No need to wait! He'll pass and be at the top of his class as usual."

Mukhlif laughed and shook my hands with pride, a broad smile on his face. "I saw in a dream that the piggy bank has more than a dinar."

I yelled, "Impossible!"

"I told you, I saw it in a dream. My dreams are real and accurate."

"Ridiculous."

"Break it open, and if the amount of money is less than a dinar, I'll pay the difference from my own pocket."

I laughed. It had to be some kind of a joke. I wasn't excited about it; I didn't believe it. Sami pointed a threatening index finger at Mukhlif and shouted, "You're not going to go back on your word!"

"I won't go back on my word. Bring your father to witness it."

Sami ran to his father and pulled him by the hand. Hasqail jogged over, trying to hold his fez on his head to keep it from falling off, as my father used to do when he was in a hurry. When he arrived at Mukhlif's store, Sami explained Mukhlif's promise to me. Sami's joy was unequalled, because I had promised him that I would read him the story of Sindbad the Sailor, the Thief of Baghdad, Antara Al-Absi, Saif bin Dhi Yazan, and so forth as soon as I could pay the security deposit at the public library. Hasqail sat on a bench outside Mukhlif's store while Sami and I went into the depths of the shop. Mukhlif brought out a sheepskin with the fleece side down and put the piggy bank on it. Then Sami ran and brought a hammer from his father's store. Mukhlif handed me the hammer and said, "You break it."

I raised the hammer to hit it, but I hesitated. The piggy bank had been with me for many days, and despite what Mukhlif had said, I was sure it didn't contain the amount I wanted. So I didn't really want to break it, and I hit it very weakly. It moved but didn't break. Sami yelled, "What's the matter with you? Are you scared of it?" Then he grabbed the hammer from me and whacked it, and the coins scattered all over the sheepskin.

Scooping up a handful, Hasqail said, "Let's sort them by denomination." In those days, there was a coin for one fils, a second one for two fils, and a third one for four fils, called an *ana*. Then there was one for ten fils and one for twenty. When we counted them all up, the total was one dinar and a hundred and twenty-five fils. I couldn't believe my eyes. I couldn't imagine how the miracle could have happened. All I remember is that I felt an indescribable joy. Suddenly I had become rich.

Then my heart skipped a beat. I said, "The library manager won't accept this junk. He'll laugh at us and kick us out. No one will accept it."

Mukhlif thought, feigning concern. "Leave it with me. I need junk." He handed me a dinar, two dirhams, and twenty-five fils.

The next day, I wore my school clothes and went to the library with Sami, who insisted on accompanying me. We went in. The main reading hall faced us, and my heart rejoiced. There were pictures on the walls: Ahmad Shawqi leaning on his right hand while thinking. Hafez Ibrahim wearing his tall fez. Gibran Khalil Gibran, Mutran Khalil, Zaki Abu Shadi, Elya Abu Madi, and others. Through the wide windows facing the river, readers could enjoy a view of the left bank of the Tigris and the iron bridge. They could breathe the humid river air.

I handed the money to the manager. After filling in the blanks with a pen, he gave me a receipt, along with an important counsel: laying stress on the words while staring into my eyes, he said, "Keep this receipt. Don't lose it. Otherwise you won't be able to get back your security money, ever." I folded the paper and put in my pocket. Then immediately I went inside with Sami toward the records department.

At that time, libraries didn't have the card catalogue system. There were a number of folders on a rectangular table. One folder was for traditional literature, and another was for short stories and novels. There was a third for poetry, a fourth for philosophy, a fifth for history, and so forth. The titles were handwritten in ink and organized alphabetically. New books were added to the end of the list as they came, in no particular order. I couldn't find Sindbad in history or in stories. Sami got upset. We hurried over to the clerk responsible for classification. He smiled.

"There is no one book with the title "Sindbad." You can find the story in *A Thousand and One Nights*. That one we don't allow to be taken outside the library. It's a reference work, and reference works can't be borrowed. You could read it here. But I don't recommend it. You're too young to understand it."

Sami raised his voice, objecting: "He understands everything! He's at the top of his class."

The man smiled at us and then he stared at me: "All right. I'll let you have it. But you have to read it here. You can't take it home with you."

Frustrated, Sami turned to me. "That's fine. Read it here, and when you're done, come to the store and tell us what you've read."

I thought it was a reasonable idea. Hasqail used to let Sami go to the movies with his brother, and when he had seen a movie he would tell us all about it in the next few days. I would do the same thing. Sami sadly left the library. I sat down by myself and started to read. When I was done reading, I picked out a book called *The Mother*, by Maxim Gorky, for its appealing title and because the first page was easy to read. I also chose two other Arabic novels whose authors I can't remember. I got back to the market before the sunset prayers, thrilled, with my treasure under my arm. The whole market was dark and gloomy, all the stores closed. My heart contracted, so I went home by a different road.

After the Mad Dog left, I told my mother that if he did what he said and withdrew my security deposit from the library, I would kill him or I would commit suicide. She comforted me while she was helping my other sister wipe the blood from my face with a wet cloth. "Relax, he won't go through with it. He can't."

Sami, Mukhlif, Hamu, and I weren't the only ones who would suffer from the withdrawal of the security deposit; next to me, my mother would suffer the most. She loved listening to me while I read to her, especially during the long winter's days. In winter the sun set in Mosul around three o'clock in the afternoon. Nights were long, and we didn't buy a radio until 1951, when I had finished elementary school.

My mother could understand classical Arabic, perhaps from her studies when she was young. When she was two years old, she heard some boys and girls singing in a nearby elementary school run by nuns. She climbed up to look out the window which overlooked the school playground. Holding onto the window bars, she watched the children singing the morning song. Eventually she learned it, and she used to sing it with them every morning and clap her hands as she stood in her place. The children stared at her and called to her.

Her father was a *hassaan*. This was the name used in Mosul for horse traders, people who bought and sold horses. In the vast area between Mosul, Mardeen, Aleppo, Furat, as far as Ramadi and Fallujah, the best Arabian horses are raised. There were horse experts who would determine the horse's ability to win a competition or to win an important annual race in Bombay. Because these horses were so expensive, groups of people used to chip in together to buy a horse and take it to India. Often they got lucky.

My grandfather earned good money exporting horses to India. Since he spent so much time in India, after my grandmother's death he married an Indian woman. He left the raising of his two girls to his mother. He used to travel regularly between Mosul and Bombay. When he returned from India he would bring back a wealth of things: tea, the famous Amba pickles, incense, perfumed oils, embroidered clothes of extraordinary beauty, peacock feathers, spices, small ivory statues, and many other things. Also, he always brought back a beautiful parrot, which he gave to a friend or relative, because his wife was satisfied with the pair she had. One of the parrots lived for quite a long time after his wife died. Once he brought home a small monkey, not over a foot tall, which had blonde hair and yellow eyes. It was about three years old. My mother and her younger sister used to play with it. The monkey was attached to them; he ate with them, accompanied them wherever they went, obeyed them, and slept with them.

My grandfather used to share some of what he brought back from India with his relatives and friends. Also, he used to give the nuns' school a fair amount of tea, perfumes, and spices. The school principal asked him if he could bring my mother to the school. That made her very happy. At two years and a few months, she was the youngest child in the preschool. She stayed at the nuns' school until it moved to another area two years later, during which time she learned how to speak French, though not how to write it. She forgot much of this later on, but maybe that short period of time was enough to make her love books and reading.

When my mother discovered that I could read, she went to her cousin and brought back some books so I could read them to her during long winter nights before my father came back from evening prayers. That's how I read stories about characters from Arabic literature such as Antara, Abi Zeid Al-Hilaly, and Seif Bin Dhi Yazan, and how I read many traditional books such as the biographies of Ibn Hisham and *Futuhaat Al Buldan,* an account of the Islamic conquests.

When I put down the security deposit at the public library, my mother was indescribably happy. But when she said the Mad Dog wouldn't carry out his threat, I couldn't relax. What could she do to him? Nothing. Even my father couldn't do anything.

He didn't consider him as his son anymore; he boycotted him. But he didn't prevent us from helping him and running his errands. I wish he had.

I didn't feel safe until Hasqail, Sami's father, confirmed what my mother had said: "He can't take the security money, since you have the receipt with you." Then he added, "If you want, I could go with you to the librarian and explain to him what happened." I didn't like that idea much.

My mother was worried that Shafaq would go blind from crying or get some other illness because she wasn't eating. For my part, I had the weight of the world on my shoulders because of, on one hand, all the scolding I took from my family and visiting relatives, and on the other, my great love for Shafaq. I loved her more than my other four sisters. I couldn't imagine the world without Shafaq. Even when she got married she used to come and visit us daily. Fortunately, my father didn't know about the tragic story of the foundling, as everybody was hiding it from him. If my father had known he would have gotten so mad at me that I wouldn't have been able to handle it. Shafaq used to go to bed before he returned home. He sensed that she might have had a fight with her husband, but he never interfered in her affairs or those of our older married sister. So this didn't get his attention. But I was afraid that what had happened might destroy my sister's marriage.

I returned from the market deep in thought despite Hasqail's reassuring counsel. I passed by the King Ghazi Movie Theater and saw a poster for one of Ismail Yassin's movies. I don't know why, but I remembered a verse by Abu-Nuwas that was inscribed in a beautiful frame at the Al-Thoub coffee shop:

> *Cease blaming me, for blame is but an incitement; treat*
> *me with that which was itself the illness.*

The calligraphy was in the cursive *Neskhi* style, in bright pistachio green, outlined in black, with a precision attractive to the eye. The background was dark red in a turquoise square, all in a gold-plated frame.

At that moment, in front of the theater, I had an idea: I would take Shafaq to the movies again, and she might be cured with the same illness, just as Abu-Nawas had been!

Her husband came by every day after he finished his job. I had been avoiding seeing him so he wouldn't scold me. That day, I waited for him on the street. He asked me about her, but I didn't answer. I told him that I was the one who had gotten her into this mess and I was capable of getting her out of it. He smiled. "How?"

"Have you ever heard the Abu Al-Nawas poem, 'Cease blaming me . . .'?"

He got mad. "Is that the best you can do?"

"The point isn't Abu Al-Nawas, it's the solution."

"What do you mean?"

"An Ismail Yassin movie will make her laugh."

He turned on me, angry and reproachful. "Instead of teaching her the Koran, all you do is take her to the movies every day! You'll get us all sent to hell."

"Having fun has nothing to do with going to hell. I'm not the one who said, 'Ease your heart hour after hour, if the heart gets tired it will go blind!'"

I fell silent and he stood thinking for a moment. I could feel he was starting to waver. I said, "Come on, you have the guts, make the right decision."

He nodded. "OK, go ahead and take her."

"No, I'm not going with you, you two go alone."

No one would believe what happened! A thousand years after his death, Abu Nuwas succeeded where we had all failed. When she came home from the movie, Shafaq was laughing again, and the world was laughing in time with her. I was ecstatic.

Without me Shafaq would never have seen those two movies. She enjoyed them both as much as a human can. That was to ease my pain and sadness later.

PART TEN

Shu'a

They hid normal everyday news from us for no good reason whatsoever. I didn't find out about Shafaq's engagement until the day of her wedding, and I didn't know she was pregnant until her belly was all swollen up and her pregnancy obvious to anyone who saw her.

I have no idea why all this obscurity was necessary.

Engagement, marriage. These were normal, everyday life events—but coming home and not seeing Shafaq was painful, bitter, oppressive, wretched, and miserable.

Then we were taken unawares by the news that she was pregnant. Her belly grew and with it our joy. But we were to be shocked to a degree that constricted not only our hearts, but our whole being.

The world stopped turning when she went into labor. It was waiting to absorb our tragedy. Shafaq's labor was very hard. The midwife said, "We have to get her to the hospital, now."

We were not allowed to accompany her to the hospital. The Caesarean section saved her life; she would have died otherwise. But no! She lived and so did the child. All was well. My father, who had spent this time in prayer and entreaty, told us, "Give thanks to God."

Before leaving the hospital the doctor asked Qanet: "Is she your cousin, is she related to you?"

"No."

"Strange. She has a rare inherited disease." The doctor then turned to my mother and asked, "Who in your family has high blood pressure?"

The doctor's words shocked her; she stiffened and asked, "What is high blood pressure?"

When he finished explaining she said, "No one."

The doctor said, "It's very strange, I've never seen a young woman her age with such high blood pressure. She definitely has very high blood pressure." He then added a warning: "You have to tell her that another pregnancy will kill her and the infant."

My mother and Qanet were the only ones to attend the delivery. Shafaq came home from the hospital so that my mother could take care of her, and thus Shu'a came to us. Shu'a was different from other infants. His face wasn't wrinkled and red like a piece of watermelon left at the mercy of the summer sun's rays; his eyes were open, not shut. He wasn't twisted and bent like a ninety-year-old, and as soon as his face was cleaned he opened his eyes and began to look at everyone and everything with recognition. He looked exactly like Shafaq, light of complexion with red hair, red lips, and black eyes. We had no doubt he was the most beautiful child in the world, and we were the happiest people on earth. My mother said in warning, "No one is allowed to caress or kiss him before his first birthday! You can hold him, but no caressing or kissing." After few minutes—I don't know why—I placed my finger in his tiny, delicately beautiful hand and he held on to it tightly. My mother saw that and pulled at my ear, saying, "I just warned you not to touch him!"

Then Qanet disappeared all day, and when he returned in the evening he was very sad. When we asked why, he told us that his father wanted the baby named Hamid, but he himself preferred to call him Shu'a. Qanet was a religious man who could not deny his father's request. Nevertheless, he asked my father's opinion. My father hadn't seen the infant, and so when he returned home a while later he told Qanet that he would answer him after seeing the baby. When he saw the baby he said, "Praise be to God, God's will is great."

He looked at my mother and said, "He's just like Shafaq, isn't he?"

"That's what I told Qanet."

My father then told Qanet, "Name him what you please. In Islam there is no preference for names."

Qanet said, "Then why does the *Hadith* say that the best names are those that indicate gratitude and worship?"

My father smiled and asked: What were the names of the Prophet's sons?

"Ibrahim and Qasem."

"Do you understand now?"

My father's responses were always short and to the point. He made his statement and then sat on his bed, took out his glasses, and began to read *The Way of the Righteous,* stifling the many questions that Qanet seemed to want to raise.

Our medical knowledge back then was very limited. Important medical facts were unknown to us, and there was no one around who was knowledgeable enough to explain these important issues. No one could explain to me the meaning of high blood pressure, or the meaning of inherited diseases, and so on.

The doctor's warning was useless. Shafaq became pregnant again when Shu'a was no more than a year and a few months old. Everyone was worried, and so the issue of abortion came up, but Qanet's religious father, the great man of religion, rejected it because it was sinful. As for my father, he said only, "There is no sin here. Emergencies reveal what is most to be feared. The abortion should be done. Nobody should force her to do anything. The decision is hers alone." Qanet was silent. He didn't impose his opinion on anyone.

Shafaq made her decision firmly. She chose to refuse an abortion since her father-in-law, the man of religion, had said it was sinful. She said, "I'd rather suffer in this world than in the hereafter."

My father told her, "You're committing suicide, and that's a sin, too."

He tried more than once to persuade her, and asked us to keep pressuring her, but she was totally indifferent, and her belief in God was profound. She would often say, "His mercy embraces everything," and "He is omnipotent," and so on. I learned the many Koranic verses that my father would quote to express his worry.

When I think about her decision now, the way she embraced her father-in-law's opinion rather than my father's, I can't make up my mind. Why did she do it? Was it because he wore religious garb while my father wore ordinary clothes? I can't think of any other reason. And because of that, the most beautiful and brightest light in our family burned out.

We bade her farewell on a bright and beautiful spring day. The graveyard in the Bab Al-Jadid district was close to our house. My father prayed over her at the Sheikh Mohammad Mosque, and before the prayers were ended, quite a few people were there to take part in her funeral. We had expected to be alone, as we had not announced her death to anyone. But most of the people in the quarter were there. The line of mourners stretched all the way to the other side of the street. Mir'i, the setter of broken bones, was shocked when he found out about her death. He lived to the right of the Bab Khan 'Arbanjiya, a few houses from our home. He was my father's age, and knew us all very well. Unlike everyone else in our neighborhood, he had not heard about the funeral, and now came running. He asked, "Whose funeral is it?" When I told him it was Shafaq's, he began to slap his face and cry like a child.

Qanet's father did not attend the funeral. He did well not to, because I had hidden a knife in the breast of my jacket, intending to kill him. I hated him and was bitterly angry with him, as I had been with the Mad Dog.

I was silent but my tears would not cease. I wished I had died in her place. When the burial was over and everyone began to leave, my mother almost fainted, but we helped her up. The burial procedure was marked by an unbearable strangeness. I couldn't accept the fact that we had to leave our loved one in that fatal desolation.

Shu'a stayed with us, and so my mother gathered us together and said, "Anybody I see crying in front of this child, I'll gouge out your eyes." She added, "This child knows everything, he just can't express himself yet." And so we obeyed her, though we didn't understand how the child could know everything.

We were able to distract him. He turned two years old two weeks after Shafaq's funeral. He was a spark of energy and action. I cut up several cartons, drew the story of Khaldouniya on them, wrote the alphabet and numbers, and began to teach him. I would teach him a couple of letters a day. He was able to recognize all the letters in less than a month, and would point to each letter as I pronounced them to him. Qanet was very pleased. He hugged me and asked me to write in each square one of the many holy names of God. I said, "Let's take it a step at a time, we don't want to overwhelm him."

Qanet visited us almost daily. He would bring Shu'a gifts and play with him. Then one day I saw him and my mother sitting to the side whispering. I overheard my mother say, "This is your right, my son, it's God's will," and I guessed that he wanted to get married. Tradition did not require the son-in-law to consult his first wife's parents about marriage, but he was a kind man who knew how we loved Shu'a. We later heard he married a poor sixteen-year-old girl, and we weren't surprised about that, but his visits to Shu'a decreased to once a week, on Fridays only. He then shocked us all by announcing, six months after Shafaq's death, that he was going to take Shu'a to live with him. We were all paralyzed by the news. We never expected him to do that. It never occurred to us, though it should have, but we weren't thinking. When he saw our reaction, he said, "I don't mean now." He struck his forehead and said, "Oh my, I was too hasty. I don't mean now, but later, when you get used to the idea."

His statement didn't comfort us, because we knew fate would take over sooner or later. He was very embarrassed; I noticed sweat on his brow. He got up and left. My father said, "This is his right. We're not competing with him, but I would like to talk before that happens."

Qanet didn't return, but he sent his father to talk to us, the man with the turban, religious garb, and big smile. My father rose when he saw him, shook his hand, and said, "We have no objection. Shu'a can move in with his father, but we don't want the child to be traumatized. First let his stepmother come here a few times so he can get to know her. After all, she's the one who will be home with him all day, not Qanet."

Everyone thought it was a good idea, and so my mother received Siham like a daughter. She was welcomed into our home. She was a pretty, dark girl, more shy and conservative than Shafaq. The first time she came she just stood in the doorway, and when my mother asked her to sit, she blushed and sat where she was standing. She stared at the ground and so my mother went to her, lifted her up, kissed her on the cheeks, and said, "You are now my daughter, and these are your sisters and brothers. Come." She brought her inside the house, sat by her and hugged her. Siham began to cry. We were all touched by that; my sisters cried too. My mother, however, wiped Siham's tears and told her, "This is your home and you should never hesitate to come here."

All this went on while Shu'a was riding on his father's shoulders, Qanet leaping around the courtyard like a horse.

Qanet left Siham at our house. She rushed to help my mother with her chores, without ever being asked. She volunteered to cook several times, and asked my mother to teach her new recipes. She won our love very fast, and was able to gain Shu'a's love as well. He loved her as much as he loved all of us. Then one day she took him to her house, as my father had suggested. She always brought him back when he asked to return. She had bought several toys. He easily grew accustomed to his new house, and we were comforted that he was in kind hands.

Then Siham asked my mother to allow her to take Shu'a and move back into her own house. Our house became sad and empty without Shu'a. We visited him a week later and were overjoyed to be with him, as he was to be with us. He played with all of us till sleep overcame him. We continued to visit him every couple of days. When I wanted to visit him more often, my mother objected. Siham was just a couple of years older than me, and my mother worried that Qanet might misinterpret the visits.

A few days later we were shocked to hear that Shu'a was sick. We immediately went to see him. He was sleeping on a small bed and next to him there were several bottles of medicine. His face was pale and thin. He reminded me of the faces of Selam's mother and Madeleine. He woke up, opened his eyes, and stretched his arms out to us. We all hugged him and cried. We kissed and hugged him, but then he withdrew and fell into a deep sleep. Before leaving I held on to Qanet and begged him, "Let me stay here," but my mother objected. She pulled me away and told Qanet, "Don't worry about it."

The following day, early in the evening, Qanet pushed the door open and rushed in. He was pale, and his eyes were red. He stood in the middle of the living room and screamed like a madman: "Shu'a is dead!" He knelt on the floor, and began to beat his head and cry. I rushed and picked him up. My mother screamed and began to strike her face. The neighbors gathered, and in a few minutes our house was full.

A few minutes later we were shocked to see Siham. She came in without a cloak or shoes, her hair was all disheveled, and she was carrying Shu'a against her chest, kissing him and wailing, "No, he's not dead, he's my son; he's not dead." Her face was red where she had been hitting herself. She sat in the same place she had sat the first time she came to our house, on the doorstep, with Shu'a in her lap with his head drooping, her hands absently beating the floor.

We buried Shu'a next to Shafaq, and took Siham to the hospital. We went home, overcome with sadness. Three days later Qanet went to the hospital to bring Siham home. One of the doctors told Qanet, "You have to be patient with her. She's young. Thank God, she's gotten over the worst of the tragedy. All that's left now is the pain. And that in time will pass as well."

My father suggested that Qanet take Siham to her parents' house to stay for a while. He also told him to move to another house, a new place that would not remind Siham of Shu'a. Or, he said, he could leave her with us, so that isolation would not add to her sadness. But she would have none of it.

My father gripped Qanet's arm and insisted: "Force her, bring her parents to stay with her for a while, she shouldn't be alone."

She refused, and we all had to accept her decision. My father was very worried and kept after them—unusual behavior on my father's part because he usually said something only once. But neither of them listened anyway.

A few days later Qanet returned to an unusually silent home. When he opened the bedroom door he found Siham's body dangling from the ceiling fan, and lying on the ground an overturned oil tin.

That was our season of sorrow. We cried for Siham as we had for Shafaq and Shu'a. A permanent sadness settled on our house. Qanet went into a deep depression. Had he not been religious, he would have killed himself, like Siham. He was never again the same; his smile was gone, the chuckling laughter was gone, and the joy and the will to continue studying died as well. Every Friday we went to the cemetery where our most precious loved ones were buried. Qanet always beat us there. He would be sitting by the grave, reading the Koran and crying. We would read the *Fatiha*, the opening verse of the Koran, and listen to him quietly read other verses in a voice distorted by tears. We would all cry with him until my mother would pull us away.

Later we learned that his conscience was heavy with regret; it weighed on him like the mountain of Hamreen. He had wanted Siham to get pregnant; but tests had shown that she could not bear children, and that is why he had taken Shu'a home. He had also blamed her for Shu'a's death. Had she been a normal child-bearing woman, Shu'a would have stayed with us and not died.

How did he arrive at this conclusion? No one knows. He realized his mistake too late, and began to regret it, and so punished himself by never marrying again. He died in his thirties, having never forgotten us. On the contrary, he had become one of us, sharing in our joys and sorrows.

Shafaq died in 1952. Her passing made our hearts bleed. Two years later, in 1954, her son Shu'a died, and to us that was the tragedy of all tragedies. The memory of Shafaq and her son still fills my eyes with tears.

My father was the most affected by these tragedies. He was deeply afflicted by Shafaq's death in a way we didn't expect, and her son's death affected him even more than hers. My father was very taciturn and spoke little. He suppressed his sorrows and tried to hide them even from my mother. He would welcome people—family members and strangers alike—with a constant smile, masking his emotions. I knew him better than others, though: he was suffering silently inside. He developed cancer after Shu'a's death and the tragedies that followed. A few months later, he had chest pains, and the illness slowly progressed. He passed away in 1956.

PART ELEVEN

Nour

It was strange that Shafaq lived all her life and died without her or any of us—me, my sisters, and brothers—knowing that she was not truly our sister.

When I passed the third year of middle school and began to prepare for high school, I asked my father for a watch to help me get to school on time. He agreed and immediately went to one of the traders in the *khan,* where, I believe, he borrowed money. It was early fall, when the countdown begins, as sales fall off with the approach of winter and dry up entirely when it arrives. I regretted making him go into debt and I told him, "Let's put off buying the watch till summer."

He smiled and said, "You won't need it then."

"But . . ."

"God will provide. Don't worry."

I thought he was going to buy a regular watch, but he walked ahead of me and stopped at the intersection with Aleppo Street, in front of the only agency for Swiss watches, opposite the movie house. He picked out an Omega watch for me. I took it and I couldn't believe what was happening to me. I was ecstatic. The watch was beautiful, precise, made by a famous company, and was probably the most expensive thing that had ever been bought for me.

It was early evening. My father told me I could either go home or go with him to get a broom, a loofah, and a palm-leaf basket for my mother. I chose to go with him because I didn't want him to have to carry these things, though they were light, and because I knew that a visiting sheikh was going to perform the evening prayers and it would be disrespectful for my father to walk into the mosque carrying these items. We entered the Atami market, and when we were about fifty steps from my father's store, we saw people all along the marketplace looking toward it. My father always tried to avoid eye contact with the Mad Dog, and would enter the market through a different entrance. He was accustomed, as a devout Muslim, to greet everyone he passed. That day, however, as we were passing the people we overheard more than one person saying respectfully, "The Mullah is here, the Mullah is here."

Something was going on, and it seemed to be connected to us. What was it? Zaki, a young man of twenty-five, gathered his courage, blocked my father's way, and—unable to contain his glee—said, "Who's this society lady that's waiting for you, Mullah?"

I heard my father say, "Your sister."

The sound of laughter surrounded us. Zaki blushed, and then another said laughingly, "She sure is welcome."

Zaki withdrew in embarrassment. My father never used foul language, cursed, or insulted anyone. He was a true God-fearing moralist. When I recall his response that day, I know that he didn't intend to insult Zaki, and I think everyone else knew that. We all knew he had intended to teach him a lesson. But why was he so harsh? I assumed it to be just another one of his principles. I remember he once advised me to walk away from any young girl I saw. He said, "There are three types of women: You must treat girls who are younger than you like you do your sisters because they need your support; treat girls who are your age like you would your wife, who will always need your help; and older women are to be treated with respect like the respect you give your mother." When he answered Zaki by saying "your sister," he meant this woman deserved consideration as a sister would, in order not to be misunderstood for being in the market. That is all there is to it, nothing more.

From a distance I could see a tall young woman with red hair and a fair complexion who looked a lot like Shafaq, may God rest her soul. She was unveiled, with no cloak or headscarf, and that was a serious departure from the manners of the time. Her hair was short and beautifully done, like Ava Gardner's in *Pandora and the Flying Dutchman* if hers had been red. I had never seen anyone as elegant in my life.

My father walked calmly toward the store, dignified in his formal clothing and impressive in his composure and accomodating manner. He always wore the traditional attire, a vest over a white shirt and a cashmere or woolen cape over his shoulders. He also wore a red *tarboosh* on his head, the uniform look of all the merchants at the Atami market, regardless of religion.

The people gathered in the street made way for my father as he approached them. Their eyes, however, remained fixed on the great lady and the gentleman who was with her, a handsome, dark young man in his early forties, maybe a centimeter taller than she was. He was wearing a gray woolen suit with thin white stripes. The suit was very elegant and pressed with a sword-like crease down the trouser legs. He wore a blinding white shirt and a red and white–striped tie. His hair had a brilliant shine and was neatly combed and parted on one side.

This pair had just stepped out of an American film and been thrown in their flesh and blood elegance into the Atami market, long sunk in lethargic antiquity, to drag it into the twentieth century in a single leap, a phenomenon conceived only by Darwin. Who could have imagined it? Was it possible? Was it real or a phantom? Could this happen in a city that, in 1952, had only a few unveiled girls over the age of 12? All this was going through my mind as my father and I approached the store. No wonder both sides of the Atami market were full of curious people whose whispered comments I heard as we walked by them. What could the solution to this mystery be?

What was my father thinking? Did he feel diminished? Embarrassed? Scandalized? I don't know. I wanted to ask him, but didn't dare. I didn't look at him as we walked and couldn't see the expression on his face.

As we got closer to the store, my head spun from the scent of perfume. I was intoxicated by the scent as she ran to my father and excitedly called out in Mosul dialect, "My uncle!"

She hugged him and kissed him on the cheek. She then took his hand and kissed it several times. This was the first time I had seen my father overcome by embarrassment. He tried to pull his hand away, but couldn't. The man approached and hugged him, took his hand too, and kissed it more than once.

My father regained his composure and turned to cast a harsh look at all the gawking people, who got the message and returned to their stores. I saw the Mad Dog standing behind someone, and saw him withdraw with everyone else.

Before going into his modest store, whose total goods were not equal in worth to one item worn by either of the two newcomers, my father gave the couple a questioning look. The young lady immediately said, "Uncle, I am Nour."

Neither my father nor I could recall the name Nour. When she saw our reaction she added, "I am Nour, Taufik's daughter."

My father froze for a second, and then his eyes glistened with tears as he whispered, "Taufik, you are the daughter of Taufik?"

"Yes, and this is my husband Ihsan."

My father looked at the urbane figure before him and said, "God's will be done." He turned to her and said, "Where have you been all this time, my daughter?"

I knew that Taufik was my father's middle brother, between my father and his brother Abdul Hamid. He had been a date merchant in Basra, but news of him had been cut off many years ago. His name came up by chance every once in a while. Once, for example, when Fathia, a relative of my father's, was talking about her brother, who had drowned decades ago, she told my mother by way of clarification that he had been a friend of Taufik's, "your husband's brother."

Suddenly my father's eyes were filled with tears. Then he got control of himself and changed the subject by taking my hand and looking long and deep at me, a look I had not seen before. He said, "Go with her and bring their things to the house."

The young lady wanted to speak, but he said with a firmness I had never seen before, "No need to argue, I want to hear about everything, and want to tell you and your husband many things too. You must come to my house."

That meant there was more than one important topic that they had to discuss. They turned and followed me toward our home at Bab Al-Toub, glad finally to be free of the curious stares of all the market people. As for me, there weren't many there who knew me, and I never cared much whether strangers stared at me or not.

Nour gently held on to my hand, and I was dizzied again by the smell of her perfume. That was the first time I had ever walked hand in hand with a woman of such beauty and elegance.

She said to her husband as we left the Atami market, "This is the way we came, right?"

"Yes."

At that moment I realized there was someone else with them who was walking a few meters behind us. He was short and chubby and wore ordinary clothes. As we neared Bab Al-Toub he began to walk in front of us and would look back at us every once in a while. Nour and Ihsan didn't pay him any attention, though, because they were too involved in looking at the displays in the shops. Before going into Bab Al-Toub, Nour stopped next to a large store that displayed many different kinds of beans—green, yellow and other colors—and a variety of dried tree leaves. The displays were in canvas bags, and the owner was measuring a substance made of finely chopped yellow tree leaves with thin sticks. They stopped there and Ihsan asked, "What is this?"

The man straightened up, embarrassed, and said, *"Shinan."* She didn't understand, and asked, "Is it edible?"

I began to explain that the villagers washed their clothes with it. She still didn't understand. How could these sticks clean clothes and hands? I said, "They soak the leaves and sticks and then use the water for washing."

She said to Ihsan, "If somebody asked me what this is for, I wouldn't know how to answer, not in a thousand years."

Ihsan said, "You're not going to live a thousand years."

She laughed. In addition to the herbs and beans there were bags full of colorful dried raisins, dates, berries, pears, peaches, and so on. She knew all of them except the berries and peaches, and I once again began to explain. The old man stopped measuring, looked at us, and then said to me jokingly, "Why don't you come and work for me?"

We all laughed. We continued our walk through the market, and she continued to hold on to my hand, as if afraid that I would run away. They were unaware of the people who were watching them because they were too busy looking at things that they hadn't seen before. Once in a while, a few times a year, a British or European woman would walk through the market, but those women would be wearing normal, everyday clothes—clothes that didn't attract attention. This was the first time that the market people had seen a couple walk by with such legendary elegance. When we reached the end of the wool market, at the corner where the Ottoman Bank and the Eastern Bank stood opposite one another on the street that led to the Bab Lakesh gate, the short fat man turned left while I continued to go straight, and Nour said, "Come, we have a car. We'll go home by car."

She pointed to a blue and yellow American car, very clean and shining, parked in the street that led to the Eastern High School, near where my father had bought my Omega watch. The short fat man was opening the driver's side door. I asked, "Is this your car?"

She smiled and said, "We rented it to use while we're here." It surprised me to see Ihsan open the back door of the car and get in. Nour motioned me to follow him. I did, and she sat next to me. I was again about to lose my mind from the smell of her perfume. She placed her arm around my neck and pulled me toward her tenderly and said, "Now, tell the driver how to get to your house."

I looked at her and said, "My father won't be home before the end of the evening prayer."

"And when is that?"

I looked at my new watch for the first time and said, "I don't know, probably in an hour. Sunset is the sign."

Calmly, she said, "We'll wait for him at home, then."

I didn't want them to get home before my father's arrival. From the strange look my father had given me, I understood that there were perils to be aware of. I couldn't guess what he had wanted to tell them, and was afraid that my mother or one of my sisters might, with a careless word about my uncle Taufik, spoil what he wanted to do. The thought of them going to our house was a burden, and I couldn't, with my limited means, lift that weight off my shoulders. We had no chairs in our house, not even one. If I beat Nour and her husband to the house and tried to borrow a couple of chairs, I would be a laughingstock because no one in our neighborhood had chairs. We didn't even have small stools like the ones that Sami's family used to sit on to eat. We used to eat on a mat in the large room which served as living room, dining room, study, and bedroom. The small room where my brother and I slept was packed with odd and ends. Where did my father want our guests to sleep? The problem worried me, occupying every cell in my brain.

Then I remembered the offer that Umm Salim had made me, to take whatever I needed from their house—chairs, furniture, whatever. I regretted not taking her up on it, but there was no place in our small house for any such things. Where was this exalted couple, that had dazzled the eyes of so many, going to sleep? Was my father planning to put mattresses on the floor of the large room, as he had done once before when his cousin and his wife visited us from Baghdad? On that occasion he secretly whispered to my mother and sister to go spend the night at my married sister's house, and told them he would bring them back the following day after morning prayer in time for them to pre-pare breakfast. That had been a couple of winters before. On that night my father, brother, and I slept like sardines in the small room at the top of the seven steps.

The problem was much bigger than me.

The driver had been waiting for my directions. I looked at my cousin and said, "When did you leave Mosul?"

"This is my first time in Mosul. I've never been here before."

"But you speak the dialect."

They both laughed, and she said, "Neither of us has ever been here, but we both speak the dialect at home."

"Then let's then take a tour of Mosul. I'll show you all the landmarks." I said to the driver, "Let's go to Neenwa, Tel Quwaijiq, Bash Tabia, the Al Akhdar Mosque, Al Nouri Mosque, and Kadeeb Alban."

"Will do."

She gently pulled me to her and said, "What grade are you in?"

"I'll be in the fourth year of high school."

She asked how many years I had been in school and, when I told her I would be done in two years, she asked, "Have you ever thought of studying in America?"

I laughed and said, "We're poor."

She said, "No cousin of mine is ever poor. All you have to do is ask me and you'll be able to study in America." She began to search in her purse, saying, "I can't find the card, but remind me to give you my address so that you can write to me."

"I thought you lived in Baghdad."

They both laughed, and she said, "If we lived in Baghdad you'd see us at least once a year."

"Do you live in New York?"

"Los Angeles."

"Near Hollywood?"

They both laughed and she said, "Yes. Have you been to their movies?"

"Many, you look like Ava Gardner with red hair."

They laughed. She tenderly pulled me to her and kissed my cheek, then pulled out a paper handkerchief and wiped where she had kissed me. Back then I didn't know why she had done that. We talked about many things as we drove around the city, and before heading to my house Nour asked the driver to go by a house in the Dawasa neighborhood. The driver stopped in front of a modern house that was surrounded by a fenced garden with pistachio, olive, orange, lemon, and some other trees I was not familiar with. They both left the car and returned with a medium-sized leather suitcase that the driver hurriedly placed in the trunk. My heart was racing. They had accepted my father's invitation and were going to spend the night at our house. What a disaster! I felt weak, as if I had taken a shot to the heart. But as soon as Nour returned to the car, she pulled me against her and started teasing me, pinching my cheeks. "I had no idea I had such a handsome young cousin. If I'd known, I wouldn't have married Ihsan."

Ihsan laughed. "It's not too late to find him a young girl that looks like you."

"He's not in a hurry. He'll choose for himself, he has good taste."

As the car pulled away, I pointed to the house and asked, "Whose house is this?"

"Friends who live in America. They called their family before we came and had the house prepared for us. They told us Mosul didn't have any good hotels. They arranged for us to have the car."

We arrived at my house at the right time, a few minutes after my father's return from prayer. I hadn't expected my father to beat me home. The driver placed the suitcase on the front steps. Nour looked at him and said, "Come back in two hours."

He bowed, said "Yes," and then disappeared, and I felt much better.

My parents and sisters greeted us. They had all changed into their holiday clothes, and had also cleaned the house and put carpets on the floor of the big room, and pillows all around the walls. The electric light in that room was weak, and so they had replaced it with a large bright bulb. That was the best that we had to offer visitors of their caliber.

My mother and sisters hugged and kissed Nour and welcomed Ihsan, who said, as he was sitting at the head of the room, leaning against the wall, "I remember we had a similar seating arrangement in our house here in Iraq."

Nour laughed and said, "Me, too." She then turned to my father and said, "Where's Shafaq?" My mother and sisters were busy preparing the meal.

My father almost collapsed. He got a grip on himself and tried to change the subject, but Nour continued, "She got married, didn't she?" She turned to her husband and said, "Didn't I tell you she would be married? She probably got married at about the same age I did, at seventeen."

My father said, "She got married at sixteen."

Nour laughed. "In America you can't have an official marriage before eighteen. But they all get married illegally at thirteen."

Neither my father nor I understood what she meant. My father was preoccupied with something else, perhaps a way to tell her about Shafaq.

Nour said, "Couldn't you tell her I was here? Can we go to her house? I'd like to see her." She took his hand and began to kiss it, tears in her eyes.

I controlled myself and didn't cry. My mother saved us by bringing in the dinner trays.

My father said, "You'll know everything after dinner."

My mother had cooked rice, a treat that normally we ate only during Ramadan and on holidays and special occasions. She had also made *doulma,* stuffed chard leaves with onions and tomatoes, and *uruq tawa,* a kebab-like grilled meat dish. She had baked fresh bread, and served it hot. My father had bought grape juice. We also had *buraniya* stew, which we would have eaten with bread, not rice or bulghur wheat, had Nour and her husband not been there. My father had also bought kebab with parsley, onion, and sumac. I thought he must have borrowed more money for all this.

A silence ensued as they looked at the food and tried to decide what to start with. They started with the *doulma.* I saw how they savored the food and how much they enjoyed it. When we were done eating, my sister poured out water so that they could wash their hands. We had tea afterward.

We learned that they had arrived in Mosul early in the afternoon, changed their clothes, and had the driver take them to the Atami market. We also learned that they had left Basra in 1934, eighteen years earlier, one month after they were married. All Nour knew of her parents and little sister Shafaq, who had been three months old, was that they were planning on selling their big house and moving into a smaller house in Ashar.

We children were shocked by what we heard, but not my mother and father. My sisters and I exchanged looks of wonderment and doubt. Did Nour mean what she said: "My sister Shafaq"? Was she talking about our dear Shafaq, or was there another one? It was impossible, there must be another Shafaq. But if so, why had Nour come here? How strange! Her hair was red like Shafaq's, may God rest her soul. She was also pale complexioned and had the same features, but she was older than Shafaq. Who knows, perhaps Shafaq would have been a carbon copy of her had she lived to that age.

Nour went on: "We sent hundreds of letters. Some of them were returned unopened. But we had no news of them. Ihsan's father went to Basra and looked for them, but he didn't find them. He died more than ten years ago. Ihsan has only two sisters left. One lives in Baghdad and one in Kirkuk. We visited them before coming here. They knew nothing about my parents. We went to Basra. I went to look for our old house, but we couldn't find it. It and five other houses that looked over the Ashar River have disappeared. There is a government building in their place. All the roads were blocked before me."

My father said, "Didn't you have an address at Atami?"

"How was I to know? I got married at seventeen and was a spoiled child. They never let me do anything. When I failed in my studies, they would say, 'Your health is more important than studying.' I knew nothing about my father, except that he was a date merchant. I don't know why I decided six months ago to reread the letters he had written to me. I had kept the three letters I had received from him. I was so stupid! I took my time responding, I was too busy studying, and when he didn't write again I thought he was upset with me. I began to worry when after three months I hadn't heard from him. I started writing to him nonstop, but to no avail. When I reread the letters, I noticed a sentence he had written in his second letter that had been a response to my request for him, my mother, and Shafaq to visit me in America for a year. He said, 'You are dreaming! How can someone who spent his youth in the Atami market live in America for more than a week? Say one month, maybe, but a whole year?' Then I remembered the Indian market in Basra. I remembered what my friend Samia's mother had said. 'Iraqi postmen are the smartest postmen in the world. Hundreds of letters reach the Iraqi markets daily with addresses like "Mohammad Younis in the Indian Market, in Basra," or "Omran Shadad, Al-Shourja market, Baghdad" without a street name or house number.' She would say that and laugh. I thought, why not write a letter to my uncle in the Atami market? But then I changed my mind and told Ihsan, 'Why not go to the Atami market? We could combine business with a visit.'"

She was quiet for a moment, and then she looked at each of us in turn and said, "How wonderful it is to live with family." She focused again on my father and said, "No doubt you know a lot about them."

My father bowed his head in anguish. "No, not much. But this is what happened. You'll need to keep a grip on yourself. You look strong."

"Go ahead. I guessed that something bad had happened to the three of them. I cried and suffered a lot, and then decided to bury them in my heart. I know that if they'd been alive they would have contacted me. Both Ihsan and I know that a catastrophe must have struck them. It doesn't matter what it was. We want to know the details."

My parents were comforted by her words and my father said, "A few months after you left, I received a telegram from a person whose name I have forgotten, I think it was Zubairi."

My mother interrupted: "It was Najib, I remember the name. Yes, it was Najib Al Zubairi."

"The telegram said, 'Taufik and his wife are in danger, come immediately.' Your aunt and I went to Baghdad first, then to Basra. We found the address and Najib Al Zubairi, who did everything right by us. He wanted us to go home with him, but we said we needed to go to the hospital and see your parents.

He told us that he was unable to talk to us right there, and so we went to his home where he told us that your parents had rented a small house from him in Al Ashar. They had rented the house right next to his own, the one he had built for his son who ended up going to Saudi Arabia. He told us how much he and his wife had liked your parents and how Shafaq had been the best thing that ever happened to them, as their house was empty of children. Najib said he and his wife kept Shafaq with them most days. And then, no one can say how or why, fate struck. A truck at Umm Al-Barum drove into an electric store and killed the owner and five of his customers: your parents, another woman, and two children.

"Najib had been at a loss trying to reach us, he knew nothing about us, and all he had known about Taufik was that he was a date merchant. So he went to the market that shipped dates to Mosul, where he found my address. Your father used to send the dates to me and I would distribute them to the merchants here and collect the money for him. So he sent me the telegram, and that's all there is to it.

"Najib was kind, living up to his name. He said, 'The poor man had rented the house and paid for a full year, but only got to stay in it for four months, and so I will return the whole amount to you.' I didn't accept his offer because it's wrong to take something that rightfully belongs to someone else. He vowed to give me the rent money and said, 'You're like my younger brother. I'm rich, God has been good to me. This money is a present for Shafaq.' Then he said, 'Please don't take this the wrong way, but would you consider leaving Shafaq with us?'"

With tears in her eyes my mother said, "The first time we saw Shafaq, we couldn't believe our eyes. We had never seen anyone so beautiful. Your uncle said, 'God is great, glory be to God, she is a one hundred percent *shafaq.*' He meant that her name, Shafaq, means the red glow of the sun and the pure white of the sky at sunset.

"It took eighteen hours to get to Baghdad on the train, and we had trouble with her milk. It was summertime and so Abu Omar had reserved an air-conditioned compartment for us, but I knew that the milk would go sour, and so I had prepared a powder of ground almonds, dates, and sugar, which I put in a bag. I brought a bottle of water and mixed the powdered ingredients with water to nurse her, until we finally arrived at Mosul. Back then we had a son and a daughter, and since we had been away for a couple of days, we lied to them and told them that I had had a baby girl. They were very happy and began to play with her right away."

My mother rose and came back with a bundle that she unwrapped in front of Nour. The bundle had several golden pieces in it, a beautiful turquoise green necklace, a necklace with a golden heart, golden bracelets, and three rings that sparkled with diamonds and sapphires. My mother had Shafaq wear them on her wedding day. Qanet returned them to us after the catastrophe. My mother looked at Nour and said, "These were found by Najib Al Zubairi in your parents' home."

With tears in her eyes Nour exclaimed, "I remember them, they were my mother's. My mother's! Can I take them?"

"They're yours, my dear."

Nour touched them and then looked at my three sisters and said apologetically, "I'm sorry, I'll take them in memory of my mother, but tomorrow I'll buy for each of you something twice as expensive."

My father said, "There's no need for that, my daughter."

She embraced him and said, "It will be a present from me." She looked at us with eyes that seemed charged with electricity and said, "Why didn't you give them to Shafaq? Did Shafaq have an accident?"

My mother, sisters, and I began to cry, and my father's eyes filled with tears.

PART TWELVE

Regrets

I regret two things very much.

My first regret is that I was not aware enough back then to record Al-Shahdi's folk stories about our city, which I have never seen in any book. I failed to write down the unique information he possessed about the history of Mosul and especially the siege of the city by Nader Shah. Al-Shahdi was the most reliable source because between him and the siege stood only three narrators, his father, his grandfather, and his great-grandfather, who were from a family known for its longevity. His father had died at an age well over a hundred and twenty years. Al-Shahdi's death was a great loss to the city, its historians, and its records and documentation. He was a living page in the historical archives that could never be replaced. All that I can recall now, and all that I have read since then about the siege of Mosul, doesn't amount to one line in the many pages' worth of history that Haj Ahmad Al-Shahdi used to relate.

The second regret is that I never did anything to help Selam and her mother. I attribute this to my great stupidity: if I had been smart enough to tell my father about them on that first day, I could have done something for them. I don't know what happened to them. I am sure Selam's mother died, which means that her beautiful child was left alone on the streets without help or support. What else could have happened to a child of her age who lived in a country that offered no form of welfare or social security? If she was lucky, she became a maid in someone's home, and lived in penury. Otherwise, she would have had nothing but a life on the streets, where she would beg, go hungry, eat whatever was thrown on the ground, and fall ill due to her frailty. She would be disfigured, perhaps corrupted, would live the worst of lives—and die the worst of deaths. This is what has been on my conscience and will forever remain.